Best Intentions

Book One of the Glass Bottles Series

J Dark

Cover design by Niki Lenhart
nikilen-designs.com

Published by Paper Angel Press
paperangelpress.com

ISBN 978-1-944412-25-8 (Trade Paperback)

10 9 8 7 6 5 4 3 2

FIRST EDITION

For more information about the author and their work visit:
http://thepandemonium.net

Acknowledgements

As with any first book, there's a lot of people to acknowledge, and to dedicate it to, so please bear with me. Everyone here deserves their own for helping and encouraging this book to print.

First off, this is for all those people in the old City of Heroes MMO: @kill favored, @electroidium. You two were the ones that got me into writing on forums.

To Dale, Dennis, Jerry, Mark, Damon, Bill, Peter, for letting me be a part of and share visions of storytelling.

To Beth, for doing that big first edit and encouraging me further.

To Richard and Dorothy, for poking me when I slowed down, and for encouraging me to submit this story.

To @IK Reborn for the reading of the draft and encouragement.

Finally, to Steven and Laureen at Paper Angel Press for taking a chance on a first-time submission.

I cannot express how much all of your support really means. As with all books, any mistakes and continuity difficulties are mine.

Dedication

This book is dedicated to all the daughters out there, especially Hannah, Robbyn, Annie, Caroline, Rachel, Laura, and Hannah and Kate.

This book's for you.

1

LIECHTENSTEIN. One word. It's the one I use when people have to ask me the question, "What's the word?" Heh. Gets 'em every time. Don't get me wrong, I'm not trying to be a horse's ass or… well, maybe I am, just a little bit. You see, I deal with people every day, and not in the best of circumstances. When you come to someone like me, you've exhausted all the nice polite ways of fixing your situation. You come to me when you decide to play hardball. I'm the one who finds your husband when he's spending more on his mistress than he is you, or when you want someone found who doesn't want to be, for any number of reasons. That kind of stuff don't come cheap. I can modestly say I'm one of the three most expensive trappers in the city.

My place isn't much to look at, but people keep reading all those mystery novels about hard, rough-edged gumshoes that have shabby rooms in old, converted warehouses, so I decided to cater to the cliché. My place is a very small, dingy, grungy, not been cleaned in 3 years, two-room office in a shabby, soot-encrusted, run-down part of Dayning, New Scotland. My one nod to ostentation is that I have magicked glass on the office door. If anyone happens to smash the glass, they've got to be very fast or very tricky to keep their digits. The glass will reset itself in its frame ten seconds after being broken. If anything is in the way when the 'reset' happens, well, too bad so sad, go see a doc to get your appendages reattached. Yeah, it's a very expensive piece of magick, but it has paid for itself twice over now since I'm not replacing regular panes of glass every time some idiot comes by and wants to lay some unhappiness on me, preferably physically.

I am not one that likes to engage in the rough-and-tumble type of socialization. I'm not built for it. I'm maybe five foot three and about one-hundred or so curvy pounds of femininity. I've got beautiful copper-red hair, healthy copper-tinged tanned-skin, and a set of killer green eyes. My name is Fern Fatelli, and I bet you've never heard of me. That's because I'm good enough not to need public advertising. Word-of-mouth is how you find me. And, like I said, you find me when all the nice ways haven't worked.

Since this is a narrative, you're surely wondering when I'm going to get to what the story is about. That's the easy part. I got hired to do a job. Exactly the kind of job you hire a girl like me for. I was supposed to find Hervald I. Thensome and record his philandering with one of the mistresses he keeps. The easiest way to do this was to become a mistress. With Hervald's supposed well-known taste for beautiful women, I felt confident that we'd get along well enough to document his indiscretions for the public record. The first mission was to learn his preferred rendezvous for picking up 'girlfriends'. This is where it starts to get tricky: There are other things that may be around Hervald, and there are certainly one, and probably more, 'things'. The job is to identify them and work out ways around or through them without setting off any warnings. With minor magicks abounding in Dayning, it behooves people to be polite or very ruthless. For example, a minor magick can 'sharpen' your wallet so that if a pickpocket tries to make off with it, it painfully cuts his fingers.

Like my hideously expensive glass window, magick is all over Dayning. Magick itself is very ephemeral, staying in place only as long as the caster concentrates on it. Or, if you want to have something operate independently, you have to imbue it with 'other' traits, the easiest being a piece of yourself, the more ruthless sorts using somebody else to fuel the spells. A third way is by a long, tiring, boring, and occasionally dangerous ritual, where you 'persuade' the loose and wildly unpredictable power to actually prefer a certain location, habit, action, reaction, etc. *ad nauseam*. The last way, and undoubtedly the one that's the strongest, magick-wise, is to appeal to the powers. These are incredibly powerful magickal beings. Call them what you will, they can give parts of themselves away for years and still be so strong that you'd never know that they've given away anything. Personal opinion is that the farther away from me they are, the better I feel.

But back to the main tale: Hervald. Finding Hervald on an evening was easy. All you had to do was look for a lively bar with lovely waitresses, and you'd be certain that Hervald would be there eventually. Now I'm not trying to make Hervald out as a complete party animal. I don't have to. He did that himself. But he was a smart party animal. He had friends that knew more about the places than he did, and they knew when to play, and when to stay away. He was, in a word, particular. He liked upscale, which made my job a lot easier. If he was a man who liked seedy dives, there's hundreds to choose from. Upscale is much more exclusive, and that meant there were way fewer places to check out. I got lucky on the second bar of the night. I could see why Hervald had avoided trouble before. He had his eyes out for trouble. And a second pair belonging to an *Imrit*.

Imrits are good for that. They're denizens of the outer reaches, or 'dimensions' as the science guys call them. They look like a badly drawn lop-eared rabbit. Kind of round and fuzzy, with odd lumpy parts here and there, with a grey and white color that blends together. They are like rabbits, meaning that they propagate fast and everything likes to eat them. They have to be alert to avoid being eaten. It is that quality which makes them so good at reading a room. If there is tension, anger, or some trace of stress, they pick up on it fast, and are first out the door after delivering the warning. But it was the 'other thing' that made me start to wonder what I had gotten into.

That other thing was a *Wurmling*. No no no no, not a 'wyrmling', as in baby dragon for the unlettered out there, or a 'wormling' as in small earthworm or flatworm. This was a *Wurmling*, a foot-tall two-foot-long semi-amorphous predator. Looking at one, you might get the idea of one of those cartoon musical clarinets that wander cutely around on four legs, and you'd be partly right. It does have four legs, at times. Other times, it may be six if it wants traction. It hunts by cocking its legs like a compressed 'L', and throwing itself explosively at its prey.

When the *Wurmling* hits its target, the body squashes almost flat like a cartoon character hitting a brick wall. This is it getting ready to do unto the target big-time. It stiffens its body to create a suction then, rapidly vibrating its body, bores right through the flesh and organs of its target. It makes a hole front to back, just like coring an apple. Needless to say, the process hurts a lot, and worse, the coring action does the same to your spirit or soul, whichever word you prefer. It's one of the many things that prey on *Imrits*. Hervald had one of these vile killers with him, barely visible, in his coat pocket. I only saw it when it poked its head out, and aimed it hungrily at the *Imrit* on Hervald's shoulder. The *Imrit* shivered in fear, trying to leap away from Hervald, but the spell he'd used apparently didn't let it run like hell, which it so clearly wanted to do.

Me, being the smart girl that I am, did not want any introduction to those critters. The *Imrit* I could fool with some emotional preparation and good acting skills, but the *Wurmlings* don't charm, they are pure attack animals. If I was going to get near Hervald, I'd need a plan to cover my cute little ass if, and most likely when, things got rough. *Wurmlings* are not the top predator in their part of the outer reaches, but they're probably the most tractable and easy to bargain with. Feed them a neighbor's pet dog, cat, or the like, and they're willing to be your partner for a while. Keep them in small animals and they'll stick around and be very happy to cover your philandering ass, or Hervald's ass in this case. I would need a good piece of magick, or better yet, science to deal with them.

Magick and Science are antagonistic metaphysically, but not mutually exclusive. I am one of those who is not really magickally gifted, nor am I a scientific genius, but I can use either one as necessary. Most people prefer to use Magick, as it is easy, flexible, and usually, free. Science takes discipline to master, everything used is of created components based upon known physical principles and natural laws. The upside to science is that you don't have to understand or think about how to form the spell and how much power you want in it, as science gives results now. To explain this, I could zap you with a lightning bolt, but it takes time to set up and you might have just enough time to get out of my range or to attack me. With science, I get a pistol and then it's just point and pull the trigger, no thought required. But science takes longer to prepare. So trade-offs all around.

But I'm lecturing again, bad habit, makes people think about you and that you may be smarter than you look. I like cultivating the 'vacuous babe' personality. Men are so convinced by my dumb bimbo act that I could ask them the most delicate questions and they'd spill their guts without a thought. You'd think some guys would be a little more perceptive, but no one has yet. Normally, I hate the stereotype, but not when it works so good.

Hervald was at the second bar I'd checked. Ironically enough, the place was called 'Culture Club'. It was an upscale location that catered to people with more money than sense. Once through the shiny stainless steel doors, you found all sorts of Dayning's, and Halifax's, affluent society mixing with all sorts of people and beings that want to bask in the societal limelight, spend someone else's money, and pitch their latest scam to a rich target. He'd walked in with two friends whom he left when he saw me lounging next to the bar, fending off a drunk.

The guy had decided that being drunk excused bad behavior, and because I seemed to be looking for company (I was), I was looking for him (I wasn't). I gave Hervald a quick, pleading glance as he leaned in closer and tried to convince me to go back to his 'room'. Hervald stepped up, and let the man 'see' the *Wurmling*, which focused on the man like a starving dog focuses on a steak. The guy paled, then hurried off, leaving me and Hervald, who shushed the hissing *Wurmling*, banishing it back to his pocket. The *Imrit* remained clamped on his shoulder, by the spell, twitching spasmodically as it tried to get away from the predator, and couldn't.

Her reached up, brushing his hair back as he smiled, his eyes going down, then back up, checking me over. His eyes rose to meet mine. I could see, and feel, why he'd gotten such a reputation. His features were magnetic, with piercing blue eyes and tanned mocha skin. His hand was warm and confident as it rested on my knee. He kept his dark hair perfectly coiffed. I wanted to run my fingers through it. I ordered a shot of Irish Cream, and Hervald ordered a kamikaze. As we sipped (in my case) and drank (in his) we got to chatting. This was when another cliché took place.

Hervald was a typical guy, looking at and talking to my chest rather than my eyes. After a short flirty while, I heard those words I was looking for. "So, how about you an' me go someplace a little more private?"

"Why Mr. Thensome, are you suggesting we go back to your place and fuck like mad monkeys on the kitchen table?" It was totally worth it to see him nearly choke on that kamikaze.

Instead of his place, he escorted me back to a small hotel on the edge of the more 'civilized' section of town, where they didn't charge you by the hour. I had my sometimes partner, Zhirk, follow us to the hotel. Zhirk is a great guy. A Troll, and a touch over eight feet tall, he was able to blend in the background better than you'd think possible. Zhirk did have a way with small deception magicks. To say it is disconcerting to see an eight-foot tall troll appear out of nowhere is an understatement. Combine that for Zhirk's penchant for large trench coats, and high intensity persuasion, the effect is extremely attention-getting when he wants it. He was intelligent, scary as all get out, and loyal to his friends, of which I was lucky enough to be one.

I pulled the sultry yet shy minx routine, and waited for 'hunky Hervy' to head into the bathroom. The *Wurmling* thankfully stayed in Hervald's coat hung in the closet. The *Imrit* tried to wail. The spell kept it locked on his coat shoulder. I could see its mouth work, but no sound came out. Gee, Hervald must not like hearing about trouble all the time. Lucky me.

I pulled the mini-cam from my purse and set it on the telephone stand by the entrance, so it covered the room. When I pulled the insulted girl routine, I wanted to be able to snag it fast on my way out. Hervald came back into the room and I was surprised to see he had not gotten undressed as I had thought he was planning to do. He was just as obviously surprised that I had not disrobed and was waiting for him in bed.

"What's this now?" he questioned. The *Imrit* twitched and wailed soundlessly, getting more panicky as Hervald's surprise shifted to suspicion. I had to divert his attention.

"Oh, I was just waiting for the audience to get back," I said in my best sexy bimbo tone. "I thought you might like a show before we got to the fun part."

His eyes got a gleam to them and I heard his throat catch a bit.

"Well, that's fine by me honey, you just let me settle right here and I'll be ready." He sauntered over to the bed, and slipped something under the cover. It was a slight movement and if I hadn't already been concentrating on him, I would've missed it. Smooth this guy, I looked him over again, and saw a few things I missed before.

He was very controlled. Even when he was aroused like he was, there was no quiver to him at all. The lump barely visible near his left arm-pit talked of either a small weapon in a small holster or a magickal surprise of some kind. When in doubt go for the nastiest thing you can think of, so I assumed pistol. Magick would be slow and this close, the pistol could be out and shooting before the first syllable of a spell was spoken. I moved to the window, where I hoped I was silhouetted. Zhirk, should be where he would see me, so if something happened he could get up here fast.

I leaned back, and began a languid, slow unbuttoning of my shirt. I hadn't worn any bra and, as I got to the last button, I let the shirt hang loose over my breasts. He started to lean forward, but there was something about his movements that raised alarms in the back of my head. I got a mental image picture of two lions getting ready to pounce on each other's rear, and wondered who was playing whom, but the job was to catch him *in flagrante delecto*, and, like I said, you want to play hardball you come to me. I began to sway my hips slowly and started to unzip my pants.

His voice came thick and filled with desire, "Come here girl, I have something for you."

I swayed over to him, alert as he reached his hand under the bed cover. "What's that?" I questioned as I moved to just out of reach.

Something was up, and the way the *Imrit* was suddenly paralyzed in the open closet, it was because of him more than me. He was tensing up, getting ready to pounce. It was time to bail.

I turned off the charm, stepped further back, and indicated the closet. "What's with it, huh?" I said, deliberately getting angry. "You planning something, huh? Well, plan it with yourself 'cause I'm outta here!"

I turned to the door and zipped my pants back up, and heard a quick shuffle behind me. I dropped and rolled back toward him. He had been right behind me, and couldn't stop his momentum. He tripped over me, slamming to the floor. I rolled to my feet, scrambling for the door. I had made sure I was last in so the door was unlocked. I snatched at the mini-cam and knocked it to the floor. I stopped, and then started to run again as I was sure he was on top of me.

"Zhirk!" I screamed out the open door. "Zhirk!"

I looked behind me, and stopped. There was no movement, no sound coming from Hervald. Zhirk thundered up the stairs and charged through the room, his twelve-gauge seeking a target. He relaxed marginally when he saw me, and swung the shotgun to cover the collapsed and unmoving Hervald.

"By the Outsiders, Fern, what did you do, give him a heart attack?" he asked me with a touch of amusement.

"No, I dived into his legs when he tried to grab me," I replied.

Zhirk turned Hervald over. A small bottle clung to the side of his hand. I squatted down to look at it. It was made of an odd-looking metallic glass. A small cork stopper lay on the floor.

I looked Hervald over carefully. His eyes were open and glassy. Spittle dribbled from the corner of his mouth, dripping to the carpet and soaking slowly in. His chest rose and fell shallowly, so he wasn't dead. It was like no one was home at all. I looked again at the bottle and sounded out a small spell to see if magick was active. The moment the spell activated, I had to douse it, as the power nearly burned my eyes from their sockets. The bottle was glowing like a small sun. What the hell was going on here?

2

Z HIRK, BEING THE LAW-ABIDING SORT THAT HE IS, called the police as I was looking Hervald over. The police showed in a blink of yellow-green light that blinded me momentarily. My eyes still had after-images from looking at the bottle, so this lanced right into my brain and it hurt.

"Hey there Shorty. Funny seeing you here," a sultry voice said. I groaned inwardly. "Now how are you all mixed in this?"

Zhirk saved me from a smart-mouth remark. "Guy was her mark — she was supposed to catch him foolin' around."

Fawn smirked. "No fooling huh? Come here and give Fawny a hug you big troll boy you."

The cops were just as surprised as I was. My sister, Fawn, looks like your stereotypical Amazon woman. Six feet of blonde-haired, blue-eyed, tanned babe straight from the R-rated DVDs. She is the real thing and usually comes with a chip-on-the-shoulder attitude. Not tonight however, which threw me a bit. Usually she's on me for one thing or another. After my sister got a big hug from Zhirk, she looked back to me.

"This one went funny didn't it?" she commented as the merriment faded from her eyes. She got the serious look going, the one that promised a long time in debriefing if we didn't talk straight right now.

"How the hell are you too, sis? Nice to see you again. Let's see, it's been oh, three years since my last confession," I retorted and watched her cop eyes go flat and empty.

I'd done it now. Fawn would have to roust me or really lose respect. Me and my smart mouth. Zhirk solved it for both of us. He picked me up and tossed me to the police magicker.

"Take her out of here," said my sister, as she turned back to talk to Zhirk while the magicker and I faded from view as the officer stepped through the summoned portal back to the police station.

Let me tell you the drunk tank is not a fun place to hang out when you're sober. It's not so bad, I suppose, if you're drunk. But they throw all the drunks in the tank, male, female, elf, troll, troykin, hamref, you name it. If their race drinks, they are represented here. Being female bought me a little room in the tank, but guys are guys in any species and soon I was getting a number of speculative looks from the slowly sobering drunks. Screw 'em, which is probably what they wanted to do anyway. I waited quietly in my corner for the officer to lead me to the interrogation, excuse me, the debriefing room. After about three hours, four come-ons, and about sixteen leers from the male population, they came down and led me off.

I was placed in the dreary grey 'interview' room with my sister, and another officer. The new face had a tag on his left chest. Anderson. He was the interrogation magicker. Fawn indicated the chair that I was to sit in, and I plonked myself down and stared at the magicker, waiting for what was going to come next.

"Now just relax and concentrate on the events this evening." He looked at me hard.

Darling sis had apparently warned the officer about my literal attitude. I settled back and tried to concentrate on Hervald. I watched myself enter the club, get picked up by Hervald, and go to the hotel. I ran through the events four times mentally. After he was satisfied that I wasn't trying to concoct memories, Officer Anderson dropped the spell.

My head immediately began pounding. Memory-sifting spells do that. They don't actually sift through your brain, they, enlarge, for lack of a better term, the memories you are concentrating on, and make them visible to the magicker and to others. A common side-effect is headaches. This one was huge. I saw the slight halo around people that signaled a full-blown migraine. I tried to stand up, but all I succeeded in doing was miss falling into the chair and not missing the cement floor. Fawn came over to me and helped me up.

"You okay, short-stuff?"

"No, I'm not." I squeezed my eyes shut harder. Getting mad just made the pain more intense. The best thing to do was to let Fawn get me home.

"You didn't have to let him do that for that long did you?" I asked her quietly.

"Yes, I did. You made sure of that with your smart-ass remark back at the hotel. Remember, darling sister?"

The chip was firmly in place back on her shoulder. "If you're gonna do this stuff, at least you were smart enough to have that lug Zhirk covering your puny ass," she said, clearly exasperated. "Or are you looking to get minced into tiny pieces?"

"I love you too, sis. Now shut up please. This migraine is real hard-core right now," I whispered. "Just take me home and black the windows out will you? I really need to get into a nice dark bed until this goes away."

A thought surfaced in the pain. One of Hervald, with his glassy eyes staring. "Fawn, what happened to that guy anyways? It was like no one was home." With all the 'fun' distractions, I had forgotten about Hervald.

"No one is home, not at least in that hunk of meat," she said to me quietly. "Our magicker said that his whole soul was gone out of him like you'd drain a glass. He'd never seen anything like it."

I looked at her through the halo and the pain. She was concerned about this. This was a major magick, and I was involved with it in some form. Magick is like that supposedly. It looks for the path of least resistance, like water following a channel downstream, until it does what it is supposed to do. And 'do', means anything. From raising a thousand-year old mummy to extract vengeance for desecrating a tomb, to making real boys out of puppets, to regrowing a broken tooth, magick can do it. You just have to be willing to pay the price.

That's why Fawn and I aren't at home with a husband or a family. Dad thought he knew the price. He didn't, and magick showed him what that price really was. I still have nightmares. I know Fawn does, she was only six when it all happened. We grew up with our cousins here in Dayning. We grew up and moved on with life. But we still have nightmares and we both worry that magick isn't done with us yet. Odd things keep happening, like Hervald and his bottle. All we can do is be light on our feet and dodge like hell when the weird stuff comes our way. We're like the *Imrits*, trying to see trouble before it eats us. Family enlarges the target.

Fawn helped me into her car and we drove to downtown Dayning. After a few minutes, we pulled up to the shabby warehouse office park that was home. She helped me out of the car and up the two flights of stairs to my office.

"You stay put, sis, and I'll give you a call when I'm off-duty," she said as she carefully closed the door.

I moved over to the wall and pulled the Murphy bed down. It came halfway, and the file cabinets I had bolted to the bottom fell open and spilled papers all over. I got hit in the stomach by one drawer. As I bent over the upper drawer caught me in the head. It was like a bomb bursting. I don't remember hitting the floor.

3

T HE NEXT THING I DO REMEMBER is waking up fast and hard, hyperventilating, and looking for my attacker. The Murphy bed resting on the now bent-and-twisted open file drawers looked like a rock precariously balanced and waiting to fall. The papers looked like white, square lily-pads on a pond surface of brown wood-colored water. The image then faded away and the bed was just resting on the drawers. It took the better part of two hours to get stuff back in the drawers and locked so I could put the bed down properly. I stopped and the bed fell from my fingers. I always locked the file cabinets. I ran to the front door and looked at the glass. Nothing. No blood. No severed digits. No scratches that said anyone tried to pick the lock, at least as far as I could tell. I sat down to go through the files. I'd have to see if anything was missing. But why anyone would want file information from cases that were public I had no idea. I sorted through things until I was so cross-eyed I couldn't see straight, and found nothing. Not one damn thing. Nothing was missing, nothing taken, nothing added.

I couldn't figure it out, but I knew someone who could. Over the past nine years I've been doing this, I've run into a lot of odd people, and Rynun had to be near the top of the list. He was a *Geowludmosiseg*, one of the little people who inhabited the area since as far back as legends can tell. Rynun, not his real name since that is so long and complex I don't know how to say it, had decided, or been forced to (the story changes each time I ask) enter Dayning and live with 'us' here.

He, depending on your point of view, either failed miserably or succeeded brilliantly. He lived in the alley alongside the office building, and from what I could tell, drank anything that came into his hands. He was never sober enough for a straight answer, to walk a straight line, or talk without every fourth or fifth word being belched. But there was something about him that people liked. No mistake though, he knew things that most people didn't, and if you brought the proper persuasion along, he was a gold mine of information.

I walked down the dingy block to the corner where Klaus's liquor shop was. Klaus was a crotchety old guy, and the local bookie for illegal betting. Every corner in town had someone like Klaus, and, if he got busted and put away, there'd be another, who might be worse than him, waiting for his turn to do.

I pushed the door open, the little bell just above the door tinkling as the door brushed it, and went in. The warmth of the store felt good. Klaus looked up from behind the cashier's counter. "For you or the rug?" he asked. "A bottle of Rosé." I'd not given him anything sweet in a while, so he'd probably like the treat. I laid the cash on the counter and waited while Klaus put the bottle in a brown bag, and handed it to me. He kept the change.

I walked back to the alley and looked for Rynun. I'd taken two steps when I froze as the lowest, loudest, nastiest sounding growl I have ever heard started up behind me. My hair tried to stand up and I just about wet myself. I tried to scream, but all that came out was "eep," barely above a mouse squeak. Rynun lost it and started laughing behind me, and just about lost his head as I barely managed to repress the urge to kick him as hard as I could.

"Oh, by Coyote's black whisk-belch-ers Fernie, than-uuuuurp-kyou. That was fun." The last was followed by a huge burp that sounded like a foghorn, and nearly as loud.

"All-uuuurrrp-llll right, what's u-u-u-uuuurrrp-ncle Ry s'posed to tell?" Bleary-eyed, he missed the proffered bottle twice before he managed to grab it.

"I think my place was tossed and someone was looking for something in it, thought you might like to earn another one of those," I said, barely able to watch as he just opened his mouth and shoved the bottle in about of a third of its length and rotated his head rapidly in a circle. The wine followed suit, and a wine whirlpool formed in the bottle that disappeared into Rynun in a matter of seconds. He pulled the bottle back out his mouth and handed the empty thing to me.

"All you have to do is check my place over and tell me what you think happened." I straightened and looked at him.

"Buuuuurrr-aaaap's easy Fer, I did," he said, slurring the words almost together.

I blinked. "What you? You tossed my apartment?" I was starting to do a quick burn towards mad. I liked the little runt, but no one likes to have their place invaded. I glared at the little brown man. "So how did you get in? I didn't see any blood, no pick scratches, so how'd you do it Houdini?"

19

"Awwwuuurpthas easy, the guy threuuuuurrrp me throuuubbeeeellchh the glasshic," he said guilelessly. "Uuurrrp-fixes itshhheeebeeeelchff you know… noooouuurrrp p-p-p-prroobburrrrplem. I juuurrrpst op-p-peurrrpend the doorrrraapp for him," he belched.

I hadn't thought of something like that. Find a small guy and toss him through the glass. It breaks, and resets itself. After it's done just open the door because you are on the inside. Crap, I was going to have to get new locks with keys for both sides of the door. Okay, that was unexpected.

"Rynun, you remember what the guy looked like?" I queried.

He'd seen the guy and he had to bribe Rynun the same way I did. If I could get a description, I could get it to Fawn and she could see if the guy was in the crimes database.

"Yeeahhhuuurrp. Big, biggerrrrup than me," he said. "T-T-Tallerrruuurrp 'an you too-o-o." He finished his thought. "B-B-Ballllch-d as a shhhhhuuurrp-aved bu-uurrp-tt. Ha-uuurp-d a du-uuurp-ster on."

"Can you draw me a picture of him? Without it catching fire from all the alcohol?" I questioned. This was getting nowhere, and I was giving attitude. I was pissed.

"Su-uuurp-re, here." He murmured something below his alcoholic breath.

There was a slight flash of magick and he handed me a four-by-four inch, incredibly detailed face drawing of a bald guy with pointed ears and a horizontal scar on his chin, with large sunglasses over his eyes and a turned up collar on a long coat of some kind.

"This him, you're certain?" I squinted at the picture.

"Yeah-uuurp," he said and reached for the other bottle. "Gimme."

I gave it to him, and watched a repeat of the first performance, and took the empties back to Klaus. Hey, I may be well-off, but Rynun isn't so polite as to toss stuff in trash receptacles. He turns them over and will suck the fumes out of any bottle he finds, and then smash it to lick the insides off. I didn't like walking on broken glass and getting my shoes, or my feet, cut. Klaus gave me back 5 cents for each bottle. He liked returns as he could sell them to the recycling business on the next street over for 10 cents per.

Armed with the picture, I went back to my office and called Fawn. "Hey sis, what happened to the freakin' call you were supposed to give me?" I was still upset from the scare and needed to let it out. Unfortunately, sis was the target, and she bites back.

"Well, miss short and bitchy, check your answering service. I've been trying to call you for four hours now," she said snappishly. "Or haven't you checked that, genius?"

Crap, another thing I forgot to do. This forgetting was a real problem. Normally I have a very ordered mind, and I'd lock the file cabinet and... outsiders! I forgotten to ask the little lush what the guy was after. "Sorry sis, gotta go," and hung up the phone.

I dashed back outside and got a third bottle from Klaus, who looked at me with a raised eyebrow. I paid for it, leaving Klaus the change again, and went back to the alley. This time I didn't enter the alley but called for Rynun from the street. He scuttled unsteadily out from under the dumpster and staggered a crooked line to me.

"Draw me a picture of what that bald guy was after and I'll give you this one." I gestured towards the bottle.

"Deal-uurp," he said.

Again there was a small flash of magick and he handed me a three by six picture of... me. Or more correctly, a picture of me as a kid standing and grinning with Fawn when we were in our swimsuits. I recognized the picture. Uncle Todd took it about a year after Dad and Mom died. He said it was the first time we'd smiled after that happened.

"Where did you see this picture? I don't have it!"

"You-uuurp asked, I sho-oooorp-wed ya," he said. "Gimme."

I gave him the bottle and didn't even bother to take the empty back to Klaus. Why would anyone want a kid picture?

This had now officially weirded me out. A guy with no soul left, and someone tossing my place for a picture I didn't even have. Why a picture? I put a hand on the railing as I climbed the steps back to my office-apartment. The migraine was going away, but still had enough left to throw a shot or two behind my eyes. I don't know if there's a headache fairy, but if there is I want Zhirk to have a little 'talk' with it. That thought cheered me a little and I opened the door, closed and locked it, reminding myself again to get a lock with keys on both sides.

I made sure the files were locked and pulled the bed down, and lay down on it. Sleeping on a problem really works at times. The brain gets a chance to sift all the crud out and look at the problem without all the extra input. I don't always get answers, but I get sleep.

I woke up late the next morning. The migraine had really thrown my sleep schedule off. It had been two days now since my encounter with Hervald. My mind was halfway convinced that magick was trying to do something, and it involved me or Fawn in some way. My first thought was me, but in this line of work paranoia's natural.

It's happening around me so I've got to be the center. That's bullshit. Magick doesn't care about ego stroking, it just does what it does and screw all involved. To think that is to really miss what's going on. So I had to take myself out of the equation, try to look at things differently.

One, I was chosen by Hervald because I was trying to get him to choose me. That was easy. Hervald was looking for someone like me, he planned on… what? Using the bottle? Insight! The bottle! That was what he had under the bed cover. But why? Makes no sense, it was small enough to conceal in your hand, so why under the covers? I was supposed to get in bed, that's what. That made sense then, get in bed, get hit by the bottle, maybe after sex. Probably after sex, I mentally corrected. Pleasure, then business.

Okay, next question, the bottle. That this was big magick was no question. It glowed like a star to magickal sight. It hung off Hervald's hand like it was suctioned on. He lost his soul. The bottle took it? Held it? I wasn't sure yet, but that seemed to be a reasonable guess until something else came along to make me change my mind.

Two, someone wanted a picture of me. No, scratch that. Someone wanted a picture of me and Fawn. Why? Don't know. Voyeur? Not likely. If people want a picture of you all they have to do is use their own camera or a pixie and they can get it with less risk than tossing an office. So shelve it for now and work on other things. I checked my answering service and had three potential jobs to fill, which was quite a surprise. My kind of work usually sees a telephone call or two a month, not three in one day. As I started to listen to the first job offer, my telephone rang. A check of the caller ID showed my sister.

I picked up the cordless receiver. "Hi sis, what you want from lil' ol' me? I got it. A new boyfriend?" I don't like being interrupted, even when it's just a simple check of the answering machine. I hate surprises, and the last few days had given them to me nonstop and my patience was out.

Fawn, bless her, was in the same mood. "Shorty, you wanna check that attitude somewhere else? I. am. not. in. the. mood." She enunciated every word like it was a separate sentence.

"That bottle Hervald had when we collected him has gone missing. You're not supposed to know that, but I want you to know anyway. There's something creepy weird about that thing." She took a breath, then continued. "Apparently someone wanted it more than they were scared of stealing it out of a police station. It's just a cop feeling, but I think there's something between you and that bottle."

Cop feeling. That phrase got my attention. Fawn was thinking pretty much the same way I was. Magick didn't care about logic or reason. It did what it did the easiest way it could. If Fawn or I were the easy way, stuff would begin to happen around one of us. Weird little things that by themselves the uninitiated would, hell, even the 'initiated' would, brush off as a coincidence.

Or, if magick had been stymied, big weird things, like a ton of suitcases falling out of an airplane and landing on your car, with you in it. Or, to use the suitcases again, falling out and making you swerve to avoid them and you losing control of your car and slamming into the wall of a building and the impact loosening a brick on the building that falls onto a ladder, which knocks said ladder over onto a power line which then shorts into the ground and the city loses all electricity long enough for a mouse to chew through wires and, when the power is restored, short out and burn a house down, so that someone else doesn't die by slamming into said house when they lose control of their car.

Fawn interrupted my thoughts. "Maybe you ought to look for the thing before it comes looking for you."

"Let me get this right, sis. You're saying you think there's some kind of weird connection between me and a bottle. That person or persons unknown had the moxie to slip into a police station, steal said bottle, and slip out again unknown to a bunch of cops on duty at the time. That this kind of trouble you keep telling me to steer clear of, is what you're now saying to go looking for in dark, creepy places? Did I get that in one, sis?" I grilled. "That what you're telling me to do?"

"Dammit Shorty," she said, anger tinged with concern. "I'm saying that you like being in control. Take control and find it before it finds you. Call it a preemptive strike or whatever. My gut's telling me it'll be worse if you wait for it to show. As a cop, I'd tell you to find a deep hole, get in, and pull it in after you. As your sister, go find it, call me, and we'll both kick its butt."

She paused for a moment. "Tell you what. Go tell Zhirk you're hiring some muscle for a while. I'll pay his fee." she chuckled. "That ought to tickle him. A cop paying a thug money to protect a potential law-breaker. Hell, it sounds funny to me." She guffawed. Really. A guffaw. Like a mule trying to laugh with the hiccups.

I thought for a moment. Hiring Zhirk made a kind of sense. If someone was after me, an extra pair of eyes and muscle enough to lift a small car is a great thing on my side. But if this was magick setting the pieces for some coincidental happening, Zhirk might get turned into troll paste. I don't know about you, but fear makes us do things we'd not normally do. Me, it just reinforced the fact that I likely needed reinforcements, and Zhirk was a whole precinct full of reinforcement by himself. I decided to give him a call.

4

"SO YOU'RE THINKING MAGICK MAY, OR MAY NOT, be making you and your sister think that it may, or may not, be using you in some manner for its own purpose. And that I may, or may not, be part and parcel of the potential may, or may not, happenstance that may, or may not, be starting to focus around the two of you?" Zhirk summed up our conversation. He lumbered back and forth in the narrow confines of my office. I kept expecting things to get knocked down and crushed, but Zhirk was so adroit, he moved just enough to avoid any potential collision. He swiveled himself to face me, moving like a huge ninja. I thought for a moment about what he had said.

"Maybe. No one can tell what magick's going to do. This may all be paranoia, or maybe we're supposed to run around biting at our own ass so whatever magickal coincidence can happen."

Zhirk looked at me, and just shook his craggy, shaggy head. "Or maybe not and you're right on the target with everything. Gods and Outsiders, now I know why all magickians seem be neurotic."

He looked at me and cracked an easy smile. "I'll do it, but just because of all the maybes and maybe nots you threw at me. I'm going to do this for free, and you two will both owe me a marker, for when maybe, or maybe not, I'll call it in."

I swear I never knew troll eyes could glitter so mischievously.

He immediately took charge, bodyguard style. "What's first boss?"

I rolled my eyes and started to lift my hands in mock prayer, and dropped them. Call me paranoid, but I didn't want him hurt. If Fawn and I were right on target with speculations, any little gesture could trigger something. Crap.

I took a deep breath instead and let it out slowly. "Okay, what we're going to do is look for this guy." I showed him the picture Rynun had magicked up of the guy who had broken into my place, with Rynun's help, lest we forget that little point. "I can talk to a few of my friends, you can talk to yours, and we do it together," I said.

"Good plan, we'll use my pickup." Zhirk lumbered to the doorway, hunched his eight-foot-tall, three-foot-wide body into the wind and clumped over to a huge beat-up Ford 350 Super-Duty monster pickup.

He pulled both doors open and slid into the special seat, which was the front seat moved to the back of the cab. The pickup sagged under his mass as he settled himself and he reached over and unlocked the other door. As I stepped way up and into the cab, he pulled his two doors shut, and slid two latches in place that locked the doors together.

"We talk to your people first. Mine are a bit out of touch where we might be needing to look, so I figure yours are a better first choice."

"Yasa ma'am. Yasa, ah knows where to go I do," Zhirk said in a very gravelly, cheesy accent that set my teeth on edge.

"If there was someone PC in this truck, they'd be sorely tempted to really hurt you."

"Lucky for me there isn't," he said back at me, and twisted the key in the ignition switch. The engine roared to life, and the truck shook to the rumble of three hundred mechanical horse-power under the dented hood. "Shall we motor-vate?"

The first stop would be like most of the others on Zhirk's 'buddy' list. Bars. All night bars. Strip bars, party bars, beer bars, magick bars. Wherever anyone would go to get themselves moderately, or seriously, sideways to normal and sober, that was where we went. I met a lot of different sorts. Seedy and down-on-their-luck fairy winos. Elf-gangs that eyed me the way a hungry cat would a bird. The scary, lazy-looking apex predators like the Orc named "JC" who dressed himself all in black and carried a slate-colored guitar-case full of very bad things that chittered maniacally through the whole conversation.

By the time we'd finally got a potential lead it was close to sundown and both of us were hungry and tired. We stopped at Dino's for food and I tore into a steak that might have been shown a flame for a second or two. Zhirk stoked up on six chef salads and three whole chickens, with two loaves of toast for dessert.

One of the odd pieces of information we'd collected was something called 'The Anolyn Way'. It hadn't been really part of our interest, so I'd not followed up about it. Now, with a little time to kill, I was curious about it.

"So what is the Anolyn Way?" I asked Zhirk. "You seem to know something about that place."

Zhirk looked out the window at the parking lot. "It's not a place so much as a series of places. Anolyn was an honest-to-god Dragon that had taken over Prince Edward Island when the world changed years ago. His magick was powerful enough to create a barrier around the island. Any creature there was used as slave labor or food for Anolyn. According to my father, there were three attempted uprisings that Anolyn crushed like stepping on an anthill. Things looked to stay that way forever, then some magicker came up with the Anolyn Way."

He stopped and looked at me. I couldn't for the life of me why, until he pointed to the side of his mouth. "Got some juice there, carnivore." I picked up my napkin, and dabbed the spot. Zhirk thought for a moment before resuming.

"The Anolyn Way was a way through the barrier around the island, and a way past all the magickal alarms that Anolyn had set to stop emigrants. There were a series of safe-houses on the island and escapees traveled from house to house to avoid Anolyn's troops. The final stop was a cave on the island shore at the closest point that the barrier came to shore. The way through the barrier was by boat." He held up a hand before I could ask the obvious. "Before you say anything, let me finish," he said. "I know, the barrier was supposed to stop that, and it did, but when the trapped wizards that were on the island analyzed the spell used to make the barrier, they found that the barrier went all the way to rock."

Zhirk paused to swirl down some food. "One wizard got the wild idea to make a giant clamshell made of rock. Once this was done, he rowed the boat out to the barrier, and closed the clamshell. He drifted through the warnings and the barrier without incident. It was a fairly simple spell for the more powerful wizards and soon there where whole fleets of rock boats. Anolyn was enraged but couldn't alter the spell. It took weeks of preparation on Anolyn's part and he didn't dare take it down as the enemies he made would be certain to attack before he could get the barrier back up. So he did the next best thing and patrolled the water himself, burning and sinking any boat he found. The smugglers running the cave were obliterated and the cave complex was left to be forgotten."

I shooed the waitress away and motioned Zhirk to keep going. This story was piquing my interest.

"The cave complex was re-discovered by some of the emigrants who took shelter when Anolyn flew past. They had a wizard who was able to modify the magicks that made the clam-boat from moving atop the water, to moving under water without drowning the user. He was killed before he could teach others how he modified the spell. The few wizards that remained were not experienced enough or powerful enough to recreate it. This single clam-boat became the Anolyn Way. It ran in secret for years, until the patrols apparently found it and destroyed it." Zhirk paused, rolled his giant shoulders to stretch, sighed, and continued.

"The boat was the only way past the barrier, so the organization that grew up around it was always very secretive. That paranoia led them to kill anyone who discovered their operations. They did not want their one way off the island to be discovered." He looked again back out to the parking lot and got a distant look to his face. "Some tried to reverse the process and make boats outside the barrier and send them in, but the native rock is different and the spell can sense that, and the boat hits the barrier and sinks. So Anolyn still lives there behind the barrier, and no one knows what the place is like now," he said, finishing his story.

I sat there and let it all sink in. I always loved to hear Zhirk tell stories. Trolls are completely dyslexic according to the scientists who have studied them. So, to compensate, trolls developed near eidetic memories and passed stories and history down by word-of-mouth. It made them natural storytellers. It also helps that they are very long-lived.

"So when your buddy mentioned that the guy we were looking for was using the Anolyn way, he was talking about going to that Outsider damned place?"

Zhirk corrected, "No, it means that he is being extremely secretive and that the situation is also secretive, to the point he is killing anyone he talks with."

"Oh gods," I said, "Rynun."

"That lush mixed up in this?" Zhirk straightened up, and reached for his duster and hat. I grabbed a couple of large denominations and threw them on the table, then scrambled to catch up with Zhirk.

5

H E ALREADY HAD THE TRUCK ROARING as I leaped into the passenger seat. We smoked the four rear tires as we fishtailed out of the parking lot and headed back towards my office and the alley next to it where Rynun lived. Zhirk swerved the truck into a six-wheel drift and pulled the neatest maneuver I'd seen in a while, skidding the truck to where it blocked the alley mouth and leaping out with the momentum as it stopped. He even took his keys with him. Amazing. Trouble is it left me trying to scramble through the pickup bed to get into the alley with Zhirk.

Rynun was face-down half under the dumpster with broken glass from about six bottles around him. He was out cold from all the alcohol. Zhirk gently lifted him up. We went up to my office and folded down the Murphy bed and placed him on it.

Rynun never twitched or stopped the hundred decibel snore all the way up and on to the bed.

"Got any cotton or ear plugs?" asked Zhirk. "Enough of this could start to give me a headache."

"Ha ha very funny," I said, as I opened the bottom drawer of the file cabinet and got out my pistol and two speed loaders. My sister had given me a five-shot snub-nosed revolver for my birthday six years ago. I blew the dust off of the pistol and used one of the speed loaders. I put the other in my pocket and the pistol in its leather holster and put that in my jeans by the small of my back.

We spent the next three hours in the office. Zhirk rigged a large part of my bathroom mirror to look out on the alley while we sat in the office. I decided to deduct it from his pay, such as it was.

Zhirk spotted the man first, nudged me quietly, and indicated the mirror. I looked at Rynun's picture and murmured a spell that magnified the man in the mirror. I looked hard at both. It was the same guy. I nodded to Zhirk and he headed down the stairs to cover the mouth of the alley. I waited a ten-count to let him get into position just as I would reach the steps on the side door into the alley, so we would have him between us. The idea was for me to be seen and either chase him out of the alley into Zhirk's waiting arms, or follow me into the alley where Zhirk would then follow and restrain him. At the base of the stairs I stopped for a moment to take a deep breath and checked my revolver to make sure the safety was off. I placed it back in the holster and stepped out into the alley. The man was gone.

Instinct made me look up, and I spotted him halfway up the wall, crawling along like a spider. As he got close to our window, he spotted the jury-rigged periscope and stopped. I pulled my revolver and shouted at the top of my voice, "Freeze!"

Yeah, it worked about as well as you'd thought it would. The guy kicked his climbing into overdrive and sped up the side of the building. I wasn't a good enough shot with a snub-nosed pistol to even get close to him. I started to go back inside when I heard Zhirk grunt hard. I stopped, concerned that he had been hit by something. There was a thud, and a scream, then a bigger thud. I ran outside and saw Zhirk cock his arm back to throw a softball at a wildly scrabbling bald thing in black. The ball hit it and it staggered, then righted itself and zipped back into the alley.

A prodigious leap carried the thing two floors up and onto the fire escape just as a third softball clouted the thing in the head. It staggered, and then started up the fire escape on the outside, but was pulled to a stop when its coat snagged on something. A burst of strength tore the coat loose and the thing leaped up the escape two floors at a time and vanished over the roof just before a fourth softball hit the edge of the building.

I looked at Zhirk. "Softballs?! Why in everything holy did you throw softballs?" I shouted at him.

He looked at me steadily and pulled another one from his inside pocket. "Only round things big enough for me to grip and throw, plus we wanted him alive didn't we?" He tossed a twelve-inch circumference softball in the air and caught it, his hand making it look like a golf ball in size. "Hit anyone right with one of these and they have trouble walking for a few moments."

I conceded the point. My idea had been to catch him in the alley and have a 'chat', but I didn't work out all the angles. Zhirk came prepared to batter the guy should anything happen and the softballs did come close to slowing him down. Trouble is that the softballs didn't stop him, so we were at a stand-off of sorts. Bald and Scary wanted to make sure Rynun couldn't talk about anything that might link to him, and we had Rynun so that Baldy had to come to us. I looked at the torn piece of cloth and smiled. Zhirk did too. The cloth would allow us to track Baldy without us needing to expose Rynun to another attack. I was up the fire escape with a little help from Zhirk. We had our lodestone.

I set out the components, and an hour later accompanied by Rynun's non-stop high decibel snores, I started the ritual. It took an hour to complete but we had a piece of cloth that would point to where the wearer was if we got within a couple hundred yards of him. It also gave a vague direction of the wearer up to about a mile away. Not much but a whole lot better than nothing. We hadn't really gotten an idea on where to start looking, but with someone as paranoid as him about not being found we decided to do a little 'reverse' searching and try places where Baldy hadn't been seen. Weird, I suppose but, like I said, with a guy this paranoid, it would make sense that he might ask questions as far away from his place as he could reasonably get.

All this was getting to me. If magick was really swirling around us, this kind of idiocy just might pay off. We were playing stupid hunches like mad here, but magick doesn't care about logic, it only cares about the easiest way to do whatever it is supposed to do. Bugger-all the rest, as the Brits put it so eloquently.

We got a nibble five minutes into the search, and a few slow passes through the area got us a solid track. The cloth stood out from my hand and pointed to the southeast, towards the ocean. We drove as quickly as we could and the tug on the cloth got stronger as we closed in. Zhirk turned the corner and the cloth flew out of my hand and plastered itself against the window before falling to the foot-well. Baldy had just stepped out of an apothecary not twenty yards in front of us.

6

NOW I'M GOING TO LEAVE YOU HANGING FOR A BIT while we cover the history of my world so you can follow along. The writer or scribe where you're at has to impart this to you so you know why some things are going the way they're going. The first basic premise is that yes, the writer on your side is plugged into a real person on my side, namely me, and that the quality of the dictation is the result of me and the writer on your side listening to each other.

Not everything comes across well, so when that happens we'll do what we can to keep it true. But this is the story. As far as I can tell, our worlds are very parallel to each other. There's a United States, Canada, Iraq, Iran, terrorism, scientific break-throughs, the whole thing.

Somewhere along the way, our world started warming up faster than yours, and magick started coming back into our world. The trouble was that it wasn't gradual, and many, many disasters occurred.

The first large show of magick was the return of the Wendigo, and its destruction of an Inuit village in September of 2018. Another major upheaval caused a huge population shift in Canada, with the major metropolitan areas now being in the Maritime provinces. Our capital is now Quebec City, rather than Ottawa. Ottawa disappeared when someone, or a group of someones, it's not very clear, wished the city away and the magick he/they summoned consumed the whole place in the casting.

The U.S. had big disasters like that but, oddly enough, and maybe because of the geography taught in the schools, things acted out differently. When Minnesota, Wisconsin, the Dakotas, and northern Michigan were turned into primeval woodlands and prairie, the changes stopped like a razor cut at the geopolitical borders. The scary part is that they're supposedly still that way, and most people crossing into them just don't seem to come back out. The few that have talk of huge things like saber-toothed cats and wolves the size of horses.

And you don't want to know what happened to the U.S. west coast with all the tree-huggers and oddball beliefs that suddenly had magick to back up their ideas. The upside is that their use of the magick consumed most of them, the downside is that California, Oregon, and Washington all churn with magickal storms that no one, not even the modern jets, cars, or wizards, can control, understand, or survive if they get caught in one. Talk about 'natural selection' culling out the idiots. Trouble is they near took everyone with them.

Supposedly, some people who actually escaped from Los Angeles before it shifted, described looking at the city and watching it go *halfway somewhere else*. It is no longer of this world nor does it belong to the next. Renton and Silicon Valley are churning masses of liquefied ground, according to survivors. The theory that the high population of creative people created some kind of feedback, is all bull to me. It's the idiots that really screwed those areas.

The East U.S. coast was largely untouched by the change, maybe because things were spread out so much due to the huge population. The Great Plains got mystically depopulated (read tribal revenge magic) along with the Rockies. Most of the U.S. east of the Mississippi and Ohio rivers survived intact with only a few communities being unaccounted for. So food was not an issue. The U.S. west of the Mississippi is pretty much barren of people, including Native American tribes. White buffalo are everywhere I hear.

Canada wasn't that populated either. It was even less so as idiots created magickal storms, by accident or design, that pretty much blew everything apart. Only a few major settlements west of the Moose River survive.

A large number of 'explorers' have gone into these changed zones, but no one's really found anything. If they did, they didn't live to talk about it. Weirdly, it seems the better equipped a group is going in, the bigger the disaster is reported about their demise. My personal guess is something is happily killing any technology that enters its domain. The bigger the better, the louder the boom.

Europe and Asia had overall less changes than the U.S. Certain areas became, as the old Chinese curse went, much more *interesting* to live in. The Middle East is a hellhole by all reports. Apparently Allah/Yahweh decided that enough was enough and showed the hate-mongering oh-so-unholy Imams the meaning of wrath. Or, it was the Imams casting all the curses at anyone who didn't think like good little mind-slaves. Whatever, the results speak for themselves. Fiery words burn in the air and say something like, "Unto the seventh generation are ye cursed for hubris, vanity, and blasphemy. Ye have sown the wind, now shall ye reap it." Glad I don't live there.

The things that followed the initial magickal upheaval were: Orcs, Trolls, Elves, Fairies, and Dragons. These appeared and began carving out 'homesteads' in the disrupted areas, establishing populations, growing, and becoming a natural part of the world. Then the outsiders came. Creatures that were horrifyingly powerful, but also terribly limited by strange and, frankly, odd rules. You can call them Angels or Demons, as most of the population does. One group seems to 'care' greatly for all us mortals, though the word 'care' really means a whole lot of things. The 'others' just see an all-you-can-eat smorgasbord. The whole point is the world *changed*.

The technological infrastructure took a big hit. It didn't exactly collapse, but a lot of things got delayed or pushed back. Our two worlds were very close technologically and population-wise, but from what the contact/writer shows me, your technology is starting to sprint, and we crashed and burned with magick. We lost about one-third of our world population to starvation the first few years after the change. Chronologically, our calendar is November 9, 2049, and yours is November 6, 2017. You do the math. We could have been kicked faster because of magick, or you slowed because of technology. Go figure.

Anyway, to get to my home. Dayning grew from the south side of Halifax, and New Scotland is Nova Scotia, just anglicized. Dayning was the name of the first *Geowludmosiseg*, or little person, who befriended humanity and he also gave his existence to save a busload of kids from a dragon. Dayning (*nee' South West Halifax*) is one of the more 'cosmopolitan' places, with a diverse mix of races and ethnicity. It is more properly, I suppose, an extension of Halifax. But Dayning it's called and I, for one, like the name. Time to go back to narration though.

7

L IKE I SAID, we had actually gotten lucky when Baldy had stepped out from an apothecary. I think he either felt the spell or recognized Zhirk's truck. Either way, he vaulted into action, straight up. I think he was planning on letting the truck slide under him and then take off and trust to his speed to lose us, but that didn't happen. He was under the apothecary's sign and about fifteen feet up collided with it hard enough to knock the sign loose from its anchor bolts. Baldy fell straight back down, and landed next to the passenger door in an unmoving heap. Adding to Baldy's humiliation, the sign landed on him with a crash of glass and metal.

I had to get out on Zhirk's side as part of the sign had fallen against the truck's passenger door. Following Zhirk around the front of the truck, our chances at getting answers looked to be pretty nil. Zhirk confirmed it when he lifted the wreck of the sign off Baldy to reveal the crushed and splintered wreck of a body underneath. I had to go over to the curb and sit for a short bit to keep from throwing up. Zhirk had a stronger stomach and moved the sign to one side. He yelled into the apothecary to get someone to call for an ambulance.

The police showed before the ambulance did, since a cruiser had been a street over when the sign fell. The two officers took me and Zhirk to one side, then set up some orange cones around the truck and sign. One of the officers did crowd control until a second cruiser showed up. Then the two started taking down our statements. The ambulance arrived and picked the body up to take it to the morgue for autopsy. There was a small crowd of onlookers by the time Zhirk and I finished our statements to the officers.

"You, Fatelli," one officer said, getting my attention. He held out his shoulder mike to me. "Your sistah wants to talk wi' you."

"Thank you," I said and keyed the microphone. "Fawn?"

"Fern, Hervald's body is gone from the hospital. He attacked an orderly, knocked him out, and left the grounds before anyone noticed he'd escaped," she said, worry tingeing her voice. "I don't know why he'd come after you, but I think he is. Cop feeling. Watch your back." She keyed her mike off.

I handed the officer's mike back to him and went over to where Zhirk was standing. "You catch all that?"

Zhirk shrugged, and said, "Yes, and I think your sister's spot-on with her assessment. I'll bet a day's wage that you get a visitor in the next ten hours."

"Okay. You're on. But why ten?"

"I like the number ten." He smiled. "Plus, your place is in the directory, it's not like he has to really look for it. And as an addendum, I think I have solved who the thief was in the police station and why Hervald disappeared from the hospital." His smile got even bigger.

Those who haven't seen a shit-eating grin on a troll haven't truly seen amazing. The muscles of his face actually had the corners of his smile standing slightly beyond his cheeks, making it look too big for the face to contain.

"Okay Frankenfurter, tell me," I said. I was a little irritated at being a step behind everyone right now and I hadn't quite gotten over seeing Baldy's mangled body.

"It's simple really. They're after this." He handed me the stoppered glass bottle Hervald had earlier.

I just about dropped it as the puzzle pieces fell into place. "Baldy was the thief, and you picked this up when you moved the sign off him and saw it."

"Exactly, and what might you bet that Hervald could have a method of locating this bottle?"

"I'd say that's a very good bet." I handed him his winnings. If you don't understand why, re-read the last few paragraphs, and then tell me, if you dare, that I'm an idiot paying off a bet before a situation happens. I know a sure thing when I get slapped in the face by it.

Before we went back to my place, Zhirk and I bought some rope and crisped rice cereal from the convenience store down the block. Zhirk had some softballs left and he used three of them and some of the rope to make a set of bolas. I used some of the rope to tie furniture out of the way.

We cleared a space on the inside of my office door so if Hervald came that way, there was nothing that would obstruct my field of fire, or Zhirk's bola. If he was stupid enough to try hand-to-hand, well Zhirk hadn't gotten much exercise so far in that department while he had been body guarding me. He was due a little exercise, but I hoped that wouldn't happen.

I may be somewhat well-off, but most of my stuff is the real thing, antiques from way back, and it would be a real pain to replace any of it. If I'm going to have the ambiance of a dingy, unkempt, 1930's-style gumshoe office, it's going to be an AUTHENTIC dingy, unkempt 1930's office.

After about 15 minutes we were prepared and I had put most of my breakable stuff as far out of harm's way as I could figure out how to. I got out my revolver and the speed-loader and put them next to the green banker's lamp on my secretary desk. Understand, I don't have a secretary, but that small 'pre-office' is what the old gumshoe offices had, so I got the desk.

Who knows, I might get myself a studly male secretary to take my calls. Zhirk had set himself leaning against the wall out of line of sight if the door was opened. We had turned out all the lights so that when Hervald came through the front door, he would be silhouetted by the hall light.

An hour into our wait, and three hours into our bet, we heard a scraping, which is why I paid off early. Never make a bet against a sure thing. The trouble was that it was coming from inside my main office. Had Hervald climbed the wall like Baldy? Crap. Zhirk had heard the noise too, and motioned me to the hinged side of the door. He set up on the handle side.

"I kick the door, you go in. I'm too big to get in fast enough," he whispered to me.

I nodded assent and set myself to move. Zhirk took a measured step back, and then raised a size thirty shoe and rammed it at the door.

The door ripped off its hinges and rocketed into the room, crashed into the window behind my desk and hung halfway through. It had just missed the intruder though, and I saw him move towards me as I charged in. That my eyes had adjusted to the dark room was a blessing as I faced Hervald.

Yeah, it was him. His eyes were no longer vacant, but focused on me like a cat on a bird. Hervald had an athletic body and it was as quick as advertised, nearly flattening me with a punch that just missed as I leaned back away from it. I snapped a side-kick into his low ribs, and it was like kicking a cement block. My ankle bent and I felt pain lance through it. Sprained or torn ligament it felt like. Crap. Just what I didn't need.

Hervald did a quick skipping step with a raised leg as he prepared to stomp me when a bola sizzled overhead and wrapped Hervald around the waist. It threw his balance off and gave me a chance to scramble out of Zhirk's way as he finally squeezed through the door and threw himself at Hervald. Hervald had just enough time to look up before getting back-handed by Zhirk. The contact looked gentle, but the hard 'crack!' that sounded like a two by four snapping and the speed that Hervald flew away from me and into the bookcase was a solid testament to Zhirk's strength.

Less solid was the bookcase. Wood splintered when Hervald hit it, and the shelves slipped from their pegs and dumped about a hundred-plus pounds of old hard-bound books on Hervald as he rebounded from the impact. The bookcase teetered and then fell forward onto Hervald just as he was trying to push himself up off the floor. Two hundred pounds of solid oak makes for a nasty thump, and Hervald got the full treatment as the bookcase slammed onto him. He disappeared under the bookcase for a moment and both Zhirk and I relaxed. Zhirk held out a huge hand to help me up and as I grasped it, the bookcase flew upward and just missed Zhirk as he leaned over.

Plaster fell from the walls and the ceiling with the impact. Hervald threw a book at Zhirk and caught him square in the face. Zhirk's head twitched slightly, and, suddenly, I felt very cold. Zhirk was growling. I knew trolls supposedly growled when they got mad, and when that happened you wanted a nuclear bunker somewhere until they calmed down. Their strength goes way up and a troll is already freaking strong. He picked up the book and wadded it into a solid ball and threw it at Hervald, who wisely dodged out of the way. The ball exploded on the wall behind Hervald and displaced the bricks it hit. I think if it had been on target it might have gone all the way through Hervald.

Zhirk took one long, massive, floor shuddering stomp further into the room and tried to grab Hervald, who skipped sideways and aimed a kick at Zhirk's knee, connecting solidly. The knee collapsed with a crackling sound. Zhirk roared in rage. A wild slap stunned Hervald and slammed him to the floor next to me. I didn't look the gift horse in the mouth, but stood up and kicked Hervald hard in the head. For good measure I kicked him in the groin, then a second time, just to be sure. Zhirk roared and grabbed me. The breath flew from my lungs as his two hands pulled me into a troll-hug.

"Zhirk," I said, gasping, "Zhirk." The words reached some part that was still sane, and the crazy look left his eyes as he studied me. His face flushed and he hurriedly put me down.

"Sorry," he said, "Fernie, I'm really sorry."

I fell to a sitting position in the middle of the floor and tried to pull a deep breath. Nothing painful nor any torn feeling. "S'okay, nothing done," I said. I tried to stand and the ankle turned on me. I dropped painfully back to the floor. "Dammit! Not now, I don't need this crap!"

Hervald groaned and started to get up. Zhirk balled a ham-sized fist. The punch slammed Hervald back to the floor where he lay still. "Bad human, no coffee!" Zhirk snarled at the unconscious body.

Then he picked me up and put me in my desk chair that had miraculously survived the fight intact. He flexed his knee and I winced at the crackling sound it made. There was a snap, and he flexed it.

"Back in place," he said with a pained grin, and stood up and walked gingerly over to Hervald.

I propped my foot on the desk. Zhirk tied up Hervald, then he soaked a towel in cold water. He moved over to me, and wrapped my ankle with it. The cool water did a lot to sooth the ache.

"So what are we going to do with sleeping ugly?" said Zhirk. "My vote is you call the police. Your sister can throw him in a nice cell and keep him there. You've got him on assault remember? Your job? The camera?" Zhirk said with a smile.

"Yeah, but the bottle is part of that too."

"So give it to them. If he was after it, it's safer with the police than with you," Zhirk countered. "If he," Zhirk indicated the somnolent Hervald, "is after the bottle, then he has to take on the police. If he's after you, well, that's why you hired me, right?"

"You're right, but this still bothers me. If magick is setting this in motion, it'll be like a boomerang with dynamite on it. Magick loves threes, and it'll be the third time," I said.

I hugged myself and shivered. If I was right and magick was pushing things, 'third time the charm' would mean something REALLY important was happening and those involved would be in even deeper mud than at the present moment. Those involved being me, Zhirk, and Fawn.

But I really didn't like having Hervald in the middle of my floor, and the police were better equipped for felons and magick than my office was. I called the police.

Fawn came personally to see me and Zhirk, and escorted the now-vegetable brained Hervald out and down to a nice magick-proofed cell. I gave the bottle to Fawn, and breathed a sigh of relief. The bottle just creeped me out.

Once Hervald and the bottle were taken away, I fixed Zhirk and me a small snack. We ate as we cleaned up the office. We eventually had the place put back together, minus a door, a few bricks, some plaster, and a window. Zhirk looked at me as I pulled the Murphy bed down to clean out any plaster that might have been in it.

"Hey Fernie, since I'm the hired muscle and this is a round -the-clock gig, where do I sleep?"

That brought me up short. I slept here because I liked it here, and it was convenient. Up to now I hadn't thought what it would mean to need another place to sleep. Time to make alternate sleeping arrangements.

A few calls later and I had a hotel with a pair of adjoining rooms, and a mattress big enough to hold Zhirk. I packed a change of clothes and my necessities. On the way, we stopped by Zhirk's place to get a change of clothes. The first thing he did was to stick a crowbar through a hole in his wall, then he opened the door. He looked at me and said, "security". Once the door was open, he pulled the crowbar back out of the hole and ushered me inside. Once I was inside, he slid the crowbar back through an identical hole on the inside wall. Then he closed the door, then drew it out again.

"How does it work?" I was curious about whole procedure.

"I'm not sure," Zhirk said, and got a wistful look in his eyes. He blinked back what suspiciously looked like a tear. "Dad made it after he was transformed in the changing, saying that a lock wasn't good enough for security. He was an engineer and rebuilt the place from the ground up. All the doors and windows have some mechanical trap to them. I know where the panels are so I can fix 'em if I need to, but I couldn't make 'em if they needed replacing. Dad died before he could teach me that."

"So your dad was one of the original changed then?" I asked.

"Yeah, our whole family was. For some reason he, I, and my sister got turned into trolls, and mom became a fairy. Dad told us she had to go away after that, but from what I've seen, she probably didn't remember him at all, or us for that matter," he said.

I knew fairies: all the attention span of a goldfish and an intellect barely above a two-year-old. She probably didn't remember her own family. "So how did you all manage?"

"Dad did okay for us. I mean he couldn't read, that seems to be part of being a troll, but he had been an engineer, so building things and fixing stuff was no problem. Strong as he was made some of the jobs a lot easier. Sis took to building stuff a lot better than I did. She might have really done some great stuff, but she got caught a couple of years after the change by some religious crackpots. They sacrificed her trying to reverse the changing." He stopped talking, and walked quietly into the kitchen. I followed and saw him gently reach over the kitchen sink, moving a tattered, thin curtain to peer outside.

"I think that's what broke dad. He just didn't seem to try as hard after that, and he just finally quit eating and stuff." Zhirk drew a deep, shaky breath. "He's out back there, by the fence. The cemeteries wouldn't let us bury him on their ground. The churches were pretty militant back then. Hell, most of them still are," he said. "Anyway, Dad said he wanted to be close to me 'n sis, so I buried him out back with her."

I looked at Zhirk. I mean I finally really looked at Zhirk. Here was a guy who knew prejudice of a sort that you thought only existed in stories. I could actually see some of the pain that those times had etched in him long before anything like that should happen to a kid. I knew trolls had a bad reputation for stupidity and violence, but it makes you wonder, a situation like this, who really was the monster. It sure as hell wasn't Zhirk. The mood was really somber for the rest of the time. We finished packing a couple changes of clothes, and then went through the security system again. Zhirk replaced the crowbar in the cab of the truck and we drove to the motel.

8

I HAVE TO TELL YOU ABOUT THE CHANGE. Not everyone was changed, and that I think is why it was such a horrid mess. People could point and say that because they hadn't changed, they were favored by God, or Allah, or Yaweh, or Buddha, you get the picture. And the more xenophobic used that as a reason to hold little community programs to wipe out all the bad, nasty beasties that plagued their town.

It was only after people had enough of their own relatives change, that things mostly quieted down. The fanatic xenophobes are out there. But there are big, bad, nasty monsters now. Heh. Xenophobia and fanaticism have become self-correcting problems.

We arrived at the Longshore Hotel, and I checked us in. Zhirk wedged the doors between our rooms open and then settled on the mattress and fell immediately asleep. Note to all you readers over there — if you are sleeping near a troll, beat him to sleep, otherwise the snores will keep you awake and wondering if the building will shake apart. Zhirk, and I will guess most trolls, snore LOUD. It was hard to even think with all the racket, and I tossed and turned until I was finally too tired to stay awake any longer. Zhirk woke me up the next morning by gently shaking my shoulder.

"When's your client due at the office today?" he questioned.

"Umm, I think two in the afternoon," I answered.

"Okay, I'll let you sleep then. It's nine now judging from the sun. I'll go get some ice for your ankle."

"Thanks," I said drowsily, and turned over to catch a bit more sleep.

We got back to the office a half-hour before the client was to show, finished cleaning what we could, and covered up the damage. We had just put away the last of the mess when my client popped in, literally. It was, at the least, a surprise.

The client smiled, and said, "I hope I'm in the right place. Ms. Fatelli, I presume?"

"Y-yes, that's me er..." I looked at his shoulders and saw two stars on each. "General," I said, finishing the introduction. He looked every inch a General. A solid looking one-point-eight meters tall, iron grey hair, square features and shoulders. He looked like he'd been carved from marble. His smile was as warm as his rank was intimidating. I felt myself warming to him. He felt like a good man. But good men seldom came here, so it was time to find out. Before I could ask, he jumped right in.

"This is very unusual, but your reputation is known, and I need a discrete operative with your skills." He looked straight at me, as if he expected me to cut and run.

I have to say I was tempted. I deal with the tough stuff, but the military seemed a bit out my normal league. I, being the decisive girl I am, decided to stall. "So what is it you want General?" I asked. "What is it that we can do that your Air Force boys can't?"

"Someone in the military is using my family's safety as extortion. The wizard I hired can only hold this glamour for a short while longer. I work in the applied magick and technology lab at Shearwater. I want you to kidnap my daughter and wife to safeguard them until I can catch the traitor. Please make your decision quickly. My wizard is collapsing," he said forcefully.

This was way over my head and, if I took the job, it would be me and Zhirk against a faceless opponent with very high tech equipment, and probably magickal power as well. If I dropped it, well, something bad would probably happen and I'd feel guilty about not helping when I could. It came down to a moral question. The General had phrased it in such a way that I'd feel obligated to take the job, and while I hated the manipulation, I admired the neat corner the General's phrasing had painted me into. "Yes, I'll take it", I said, and the General winked out.

"Do I get hazard pay when the military starts shooting at us?" Zhirk challenged, an angry tone in his voice that I had rarely heard. "Hell-lo, Fernie," he said sarcastically, "according to you and Fawn we got magick trying to manipulate you and her into something, and you just agreed to this? Pardon me, but I thought this kind of big, bad, job was what you were going to try and avoid, not stick your head into."

"But his daughter and wife," I started but Zhirk cut me off.

"Yeah, his wife and kid. Great sob story. Give a girl a story like that and how is she gonna refuse? That was blatant manipulation and you let him do it. Well, I don't have to. As bodyguard I can pull rank here and you can send Mr. General packing, or better yet I will."

"STOP RIGHT THERE!" I glared at him. "Like it or not, I'm already committed, and I'll do it with or without you" I took a deep breath, then shrugged. "Besides, Fawn's paying for your fee right now. I pay the same amount and you'll get double. Happy?"

"No, I'm not," he said, as he stood up and loomed over me. At two and a half meters tall and meter wide, Zhirk's loom has got to be experienced to be believed. He glared at me from the upper reaches of the atmosphere, and I, I swallowed my tongue and did my best to glare back. I had this ridiculous vision of a rabbit trying to stare down an angry grizzly. But I held my ground, thanks in part to my bad ankle, and waited.

He finally gave up and sat back down again. "Fernie, you and Fawn are good people. You don't judge by appearances, and," he added with a giant grin, "are sexy as hell to look at. I really don't like this. When the bullets fly, I'll be the big target. That doesn't bother me much, I can take a lot of punishment, but I don't know if I can keep you safe, or even alive, and that sucks big-time. I don't have enough friends that I can afford to lose any, and I'm afraid that's gonna happen on this one," he finished.

I looked at him and knew he might be right. A General coming to ask me for help when he probably ought to be asking someone in the military. It was just too weird. It had to be the magick. The bottle, Hervald, and Baldy were at the police station, in the morgue, a magick-proofed cell, and probably a magick-proof lock-box or safe of some kind. I wanted it to be magick. Otherwise whatever was going on was so hidden it would be like groping blind in the dark. As odd as things were, we'd just have to play it by ear and run if things got too hot. I hoped that would be an option.

Zhirk said, "Well, how do we do this? Ol' General Confusion there forgot to send us any info."

"I guess that we ought to wait and see what shows. He's got a wizard so we might get something zipping our way via magick, or by mail truck, or something. Please god," I said in mock desperation, "please don't have him stick it under a rock in a park somewhere, I couldn't handle the melodrama."

Zhirk smiled, and stood up. "Okay, you think you'll be safe here while I get a futon from home for the front room? I shouldn't be too long."

"Works for me," I replied. "I can do at least a little thinking and cleaning. I'll try and move some stuff out of the front room before you get back." He looked at me and I quickly raised my hands. "I promise I won't do any heavy lifting, just the small stuff."

"Good. I'll move the desk in there over into the office next door. Uh, that one isn't being used is it?"

"Not that I know of. It should be fine in there for a little while. Or, you could take it back to your place when you go get the futon."

"Yeah I could." He looked the huge desk over and thought for a moment. "It'll fit in dad's and mom's bedroom. Yeah, that'll work better. It'll take me only a little more time, no problem."

"Great! I can move the other stuff into the file cabinets," I nodded.

"See you in about an hour." He lifted the desk with one hand, flipped it sideways, and slid it out the door.

As I started moving the small decorations and stuff into the file cabinets, there was a "ping", then a clatter over near my desk. Moving around the desk I saw a plastic disc-holder on the ground in front of the desk. I picked it up and set it on the table, thinking I would look at it after moving the breakables into the cabinets.

After I finished moving things, it was time to look at the disc. The General was very thorough. He had included pictures of his wife and daughter, their weekly itineraries, and a magickal holographic crystal to explain to his family why he was having us kidnap them.

Zhirk's pickup coughed to a stop below my window as I perused the information. He clumped heavily up the stairs, and dropped the futon in the front room, then sat down and relaxed while I continued to read. Zhirk's presence bolstered me. Just knowing he was there drove away a lot of the butterflies I'd started to get as I looked at the General's files.

I wanted to approach this one slow, but a feeling I had kept wanting me to move fast. This feeling may have been the magick pushing its own agenda, or a sense of urgency I had picked up from the General. I took a deep breath and concentrated on the data.

The best approach in any plan is KISS — keep it simple, stupid. I try to keep that in mind at all times. Our first job would be to look over the itinerary and do a reconnaissance of the locations. What might look good on a road map may be a total snarl of road construction, or worse, a police station right next door.

Zhirk and I discussed the best place to grab the daughter, and decided that her job gave us the best chance. We'd catch her in the parking lot of the fast-food place she worked at. Her shift of five P.M. to midnight left us a good window in the late hours of the evening.

We spent the day watching the burger shack. When the daughter's break came, she went right out to her car and drove off the lot. We followed her to a house a few blocks away, where she got out of the car and ran to the front door where her apparent boyfriend was already waiting. She stayed at the front door and talked on the porch for about 30 minutes, then drove back to the burger shack. We had a window of time, and it might work for us. Her break was after the rush had died, which gave us less exposure to big crowds.

The mother was more problematic. We followed her for two days. Everywhere she seemed to go was at the height of the local rush hour for that place. The gym, grocery shopping, a walk in the shopping center. With her, nothing was the same day-to-day. There were so many people that any overt attempt to grab her would be guaranteed to bring all sorts of trouble down on us. If we could find some way to grab them simultaneously, it would solve our problems and narrow the time exposed to pursuit. Unfortunately, from what we learned, there would be no way to do things at the same time, so we had to figure for close enough.

The mother was home on the base when the daughter was easiest to grab, so we looked for a time when the daughter was at work before the mother was home. That way we could keep the suspicion down somewhat, if we were able to make a clean snatch.

Splitting up was not an option. I couldn't do this alone and, although I had a lot more people I could use, Zhirk was the only one who understood all that was going on. I didn't want to bring anyone else in on this. Hell and Outsiders, I wished Zhirk wasn't messed up in this, but you go with what you have.

The idea we came down to was, grab the mom after the daughter gets on duty, and then grab the daughter when she went on break. We'd have to watch her for a few days before we tried though, we had to make sure the idea would work. So we concocted a quick plan. We'd rent three different colored vans under false names, and from different rental agencies. Park the third van at the bus station. Park the second two blocks from the burger shack in the back lot of a small strip mall. Use the first to grab mom from the gym lot just before she left for the base, drive to the second van and switch vehicles.

Use the second van to grab the daughter as she went on break to visit the boyfriend. Drive to the bus station and switch to the third van. Take the third van to Zhirk's pickup. Take Zhirk's truck to his place and have them hole up there with Zhirk, and pray that the General's message would convince them we were not the bad guys. Not great, but the best we could do.

I wanted to talk to Fawn, but I knew what she would say. 'Put them in police custody'. Trouble is if we did that, the bad guys would likely find out and try to kill them out of spite, which is what they'd do anyway, according to the General. Our job was to hide them well enough that when the General blew the whistle on them, they couldn't take revenge by killing the family. We needed a way to magick proof Zhirk's place, or a way to stop any magickal searches for the family.

I knew enough to cast a rudimentary shield spell, but it was really draining. Using that much of me to keep it up for any period of time would have Zhirk working without backup. I'd be about as much help as a two-year-old. I could try bargaining with some powers, but that meant either sacrifices or favors due, both of which could lead to really big complications. The powers lent nothing for free and bargained like fishwives in a seller's market. I had never tried dealing with them, as small magicks were the most I had ever needed to this point. Not being totally trained in how to focus magicks made me even more wary about messing with the powers.

We were going to need something though. Buying all sorts of ingredients for spells this fast would surely create a trail to follow should anyone think to check purchases, and smart people would. We had to assume smart, and probably desperate, once we grabbed the General's family, so they'd probably try anything they could to find his family. Zhirk couldn't go buy them – trolls may have been created by magick, but no troll I know of is capable of casting magick. It may be something to do with the dyslexia, but I don't know for sure.

I could go get the spell components, but anyone male will remember what a sexy woman looks like when she saunters in looking for certain spell components. I'm rather noticeable that way. So if we wanted to avoid detection, it narrowed down to using personal power to create the spell, which would need to be large enough to make me pretty useless while it was up, or else appeal to a power.

9

T HIS IS TIME to have the narrator take a little side-trip again so I can explain something that needs explaining now. Appealing to a power is very tricky. There are two 'sides' to a power: beneficial and detrimental. Notice I didn't say 'good' or 'evil'. Those two terms really don't work for describing powers. There are more than just air, earth, fire, and water.

Any force that can be described probably has a power associated to it, although those four are the most commonly recognized. An example would be vapor. Vapor could be something like fog or steam, not exactly one 'primal' element, but kind of a mix of the two, but still unique. The only exception is spirit in the traditional European system, which is what I know. But then, here be gods too, so maybe that's an extension of Spirit. Anyway, that's a digression.

Let's use a simple example, though, to explain the difference between beneficial and detrimental. A 'beneficial' power of water might send rain as a gentle shower, or cause a small lake to appear in a dry bowl somewhere. A detrimental one is much more chaotic, capricious, and usually a lot more excessive. Asking for rain might bring a monsoon of a hundred inches to an area, or, to borrow the lake example, you could ask for the lake and it would drain all the water from the living bodies of a local population of people and animals. Which would be what you wanted, just not how you wanted to get it.

You have to be very respectful, specific, and detailed when bargaining with a power. Any short cuts will end up being the most expedient way of answering the request, and damn your intentions. Intentions don't count for squat.

The bargaining is just as tricky. The power is going to ask for something in return. It may want a hunk of hair, or a strip of skin. I've heard of one bargain where the power wanted a Volkswagen beetle from nineteen-seventy-three. Powers usually ask for eternal servitude or your soul as the first payment. Be smart, say no. Make them take your terms.

The detrimental powers have been known to try and extort you, literally. One Wind power said that it would be easy to blow a bargainer's family across a lane into oncoming traffic if he didn't agree to exchange his soul for service. You have to know what the value of your request is worth. Be smart, say no. It's worth repeating. Say no. A lot.

For the reasons above, I decided to risk appealing to a detrimental power. The preparations are somewhat intricate, and are used mostly for appeasement of the power, which, after all, is being yanked from somewhere it lives naturally to the circle of the appeal. Despite what you've read, or maybe because of it, you may think this is where everything wants to be, the material plane. Don't make me laugh.

Here is the last place the powers generally want to be, so they make the summoning and the bargaining as nasty as possible so they don't get bothered too often. Kind of like a 'no solicitors' sign on a property for discouraging people who want to foist magazines or a particular religion on you without your consent.

Detrimental powers are much easier to summon, as their capricious nature makes them more curious than the beneficial powers. But that caprice is what makes them so dangerous, and that's why smart people, like yours truly, avoid detrimental powers if they can.

I, being smart and desperate, wanted the detrimental power. It was the best way to accomplish what I wanted for our job. Zhirk drove us out to an old junkyard that a friend of his ran. Once there, I scratched out a circle in the dirt and etched a six-pointed star inside the circle. I arranged on the six points of the circle a blown glass bulb, a burned out lamp switch, a dead battery, a blown fuse, a shorted generator from a car, and a ruined memory board. In the center of the circle was a brand-new car battery, freshly charged.

I made a second, protective circle alongside the first, and used six lit flashlights on the points. Don't laugh, it may look funny but it works. Flashlights are a version of beneficial electricity; how else do you keep from breaking your neck wandering around your house at midnight looking for a snack? I had expected to work the chant for at least an hour, but the power showed up immediately, like it had been waiting for the summons.

"Human female! I rejoice that I have been called! What is it that you require!" it questioned in a static-heavy voice.

Of all the reactions, that was the last one I'd expect to hear. It was HAPPY to be summoned? Oh crap, what else was going to happen tonight that was totally warped? The huge glowing ball of lightning floated above the car battery, which now showed signs of melting. My hair stood up, literally, from the huge amount of static electricity leaking past the circle. As long as I was in my circle, and the power in the other, theoretically nothing should happen. Yeah, and powers should be really pissed about being called and contained in a circle. We should be into blood-threats right now and arguing like mortal enemies. But all it was doing was waiting. Waiting very alertly, very still, and totally focused on yours truly.

Since I called the power, I had to be the one according to form to explain myself. I took a deep breath, squared my shoulders, and said, "Power, supreme entity of electricity, I crave a boon, and am willing to bargain for your assistance."

"I know that you are willing to bargain, human female," it retorted, in its deep crackling voice, "and I am willing to listen. What is it you require?"

"I require a piece of your supreme entity to throw confusion on my enemies." I decided to get straight to the asking.

The Power interrupted me again by saying," Yes, yes, I agree that you may have a piece of my entity. Now I have a boon to ask you, human female."

What in the name of all the powers is going on here? Entities like this just don't agree to terms. I got very nervous. "What is the boon you ask, oh entity?"

The entity mumbled, "All I wish is that I may borrow your skills for a day after your task is finished."

Borrow? "Borrow?" I squeaked. "You mean borrow them from me or borrow me for a day to use the skills for you?" I felt the entity smile, and let me tell you, having intelligent electricity smile at you metaphysically is a VERY weird feeling.

"Either condition will suffice for my purposes, now choose."

"Just a moment here! I want to know more about what you want…"

The creature interrupted saying, "Silence! I have accepted your help unseen and unexplained. You shall do also, or you may release me and find another. Choose now, human female, or release me."

I got a stubborn streak from somewhere, I think it was dad, and like a lot of people I didn't like being told to choose on someone else's timetable. The stubborn streak rose up, and dug my mental feet in, "You don't want to do it, fine! I will get another entity. Leave. I release you from our bargaining," I finished angrily.

"What!" You dare to…" was all the further it got as the spell collapsed.

Zhirk looked at me, "Fern, it wanted to help you. I've never seen one act like that before. You didn't even try to bluff it or bargain. What in that little outsider cursed brain were you thinking! You told me you had to bargain, and yet you don't even try? Gods Fern, why?"

"It pissed me off, Zhirk," I said, and felt embarrassed at my stupid mulishness. We had an entity practically begging, well, at least very helpfully inclined, and I had to get pissy and blow the deal. We had to start from zero again and preparation would have to be fast. I spun through what I knew about entities. Darkness would work, and the preparations didn't need much change. The flashlights would work for light, and I just had to create shadows or dark places on each of the six stars, to have the circle ready. I carefully picked up the other items and put them against the wall. I turned on a flashlight and placed it face down on one point, blocking the light. A candle surrounded by a paper cylinder went on the second. A closed box on the third, the fourth was a broken light, the fifth was a snuffed candle, and the sixth was a lit flashlight that I quickly partly blackened the face of to create a shadow. In the center I placed a flashlight and buried it in earth and sand to douse the light.

I stepped into the flashlight circle and began chanting. Amazingly, the entity I was trying to contact was there immediately, again. An oscillating blob of absolute darkness pulsed in the circle. Light slid off it without reflecting, or was absorbed completely. The entity did not speak.

I readied myself and said the ritual words again, "Power, supreme entity of darkness, I crave a boon, and am willing to bargain for your assistance."

The darkness answered me, and even its words were dark, like I could hear them, but not at the same time. They seemed to echo from everywhere at once. The sensation gave me goosebumps. "What do you ask of me daughter of daughters? What is the bargain you wish?" it inquired.

"I humbly request a piece of your power, for part of a day and no more, to thwart my enemies."

The darkness locked its attention on me like the entity of electricity did. The intensity was so overwhelming that I started to feel lost in it, as if feeling for a wall in a dark room. "I am willing to part with a small sliver of my essence, but I require a service in return, child of dead children. I require a boon from you as well. Are you willing to bargain, or do I leave as the electrical one did?"

"I am willing to bargain, Darkness. What is the boon you request? What is your requirement?"

Now we were down to the nitty gritty. I needed the ability to cloak an area in darkness that I could see through and catch the General's family unawares, and cover me from any potential witnesses. I wasn't sure what the entity wanted, yet.

"What I want, dying woman," the darkness expanded, "is a conduit to you for one year. A link to this world through you, so that I may enter this realm without pain or mystical censure."

That I had to think about. What advantage would it get from such a bargain? This question has a metaphysical conundrum to it. Is light the absence of darkness, or is darkness the absence of light? Both entities exist, and the question has been asked and debated almost since the changing. Others, like electricity, do not seem to have an opposite. It's magick, and that's all you can say.

"Why do you wish the conduit, Darkness? I am curious and want to understand." I tried not to tremble.

The Darkness answered, "I wish to see this world through the eyes of mortality, and sense through mortal senses. Your consent will grant me that."

Uh oh. A dangerous entity here. Not good. But one that I could bargain with. We haggled back and forth for nearly an hour, and we both got something. The entity could ride with me while I used the piece of it. It would not interfere nor influence. The time would start when we returned from the 'kidnapping'. I felt lucky that it was curious, and not malevolent in its intent. The bargain was struck and I erased the first point of the star and broke the circle. We had our power, now we had to get ready for the kidnapping.

I spent the next day getting the vans from three different renters. We set them up as we had planned earlier, and then got ready. I spent the evening setting up a protective circle for me, Zhirk, the mother, and the daughter. This one was different from the first consisting of seven points outside a circle. The points had anything that symbolized hiding from light, a snuffed candle, a cloak, a small box with a hole cut in it, a flashlight buried in earth, a candle behind a piece of blacked out glass, a book covered in cloth and covered with sand, and a paper covered with ciphered words. I used the borrowed piece of power from the darkness to activate the circle and the whole room darkened with sounds becoming muffled and indistinct.

So long as the circle was not broken, the power would stay in place and cloak anything within.

We waited until about 5:30 pm, which was about when mom sometimes went to the gym to work out. We had just parked when she came out of the building and started for her car. Shit! She'd come early today. I got out of the van and approached her.

"Excuse me," I said. "Do you have a jumper cable or something like that? My car stalled. I think I ran the battery down." She looked at me, slightly wary, but the story wasn't implausible, "I'm not sure I do. Have you tried calling a tow service? Maybe they could help."

I moved a little to my left, which put her back to the van and Zhirk. He noticed and got out of the van, and slowly moved to us. "I was hoping not to. They always charge something and a cable would fix me right up," I replied, then nodded as I looked to my partner in kidnapping.

She caught my eyes looking past and half turned to see who had come by. Zhirk grabbed her, one huge hand over her mouth, the other around her waist, and calmly walked back to the van. I got in first and looked for any people watching the show but didn't see anyone. Zhirk deposited mom in the back and closed the van door. She drew in her breath to scream but I kicked her in the side, and the breath whooshed out of her. She lay stunned as Zhirk drove the van out of the lot. I twisted her arm behind her as she started to get up.

"Be quiet and listen. Your husband's in danger. He sent you something to see." I forced her backwards into a seat.

She glared at me, obviously frightened. I tossed her the holographic crystal with the message. As she caught it, the crystal glowed and a small picture of the General appeared above the crystal. "Annie, I know you're scared and angry, but listen. I hired this girl to kidnap you and Meggie. I have stupidly

68

gotten involved with greedy, evil men. They have said that if I try to report or leave them, they will kill you both. Trust Fern. She is doing this at my request. I can't think of any other way to hide you from these monsters. I'll be alright. I love you." The General's voice ended and the crystal stopped glowing.

I looked at her as she took all this in. She was dazed. Hell, I would be too. It's terrifying enough to be kidnapped, then to be told that a loved one is in danger, and that he hired the kidnappers to save you. It just had to be surreal. This lady was tough; I give her that. She squared herself in the seat and looked right at me with a focused, steady gaze.

"Listen, Anne, is it? I'm sorry that this is all happening so fast. We're off to get your daughter now and then we'll be going to a safe house to spend a few days. Your husband figures that once you two are out of reach, he can report these people and get protection for all of you. Just hold it together for a few days. We'll get you someplace safe."

She looked up from the crystal as I finished speaking, and stared at me for about 30 seconds, then said, "My husband asks me to trust you. Prove to me that his trust isn't misplaced."

I thought for a moment. "I'll show you all the information he gave us to help with this situation once we get back to the safe house. You'll have to trust me until then. We're going to get your daughter. She should be getting a dinner-break in about twenty minutes."

We drove to the second van and changed over. We took anything that might identify us, and I used a touch of the darkness to obscure any magickal traces that lingered. We drove the brown van over to the burger shack and parked as close to the daughter's car as we could. When her break time came around, she stepped out right on schedule. I got out of the van. We'd follow the same procedure. I would distract, Zhirk would grab and toss in. The part that worried us was 'mom'. Would she really sit still while we grabbed her daughter? Change of plan.

"Okay, Anne, you come with me," I said, and looked her in the eyes. "Talk to your daughter and get her to come with us. The less fuss, the better chance we have of being hidden when your hubby exposes the bad guys."

She said nothing, but nodded. Mouth set in a frown, she exited the van with me. Zhirk readied himself in case things went south.

His 'are you nuts' look almost gave me the giggles. But he was right. If mom decided we were the bad guys, it was a perfect time to blow the whole thing wide open and a guarantee that any fight in the lot would be seen, heard, and reported. This was a big gamble, but I hoped that mom would understand that this was trust on my part, and that she believed she wasn't being played by con artists. The big roll of the dice was now.

"Meggie, come here. I need to talk to you," Anne called to her daughter. "Please, it's important."

"Mom? What are you doing here?" Megan questioned, looking wary "What's going on?"

"Come with me. I'll explain to you in the van."

"Mom, this is weird. What's going on?" Megan repeated, starting to dig her heels in.

I quickly stepped behind her and said, "If you want to argue, do it in the van. We don't have time now. Your dad left something in the van for you."

"Hey! Meggie! You are going to see..." a bright voice chirped behind me.

Shit. I pushed Megan front of me all the way to the van, not letting her slow down. Mom was in the van right behind me. Zhirk closed the door and settled his massive self on the floor of the van. I gunned the engine and sped out of the lot. I saw the girl by the doorway talking into a cell phone. I borrowed a touch of darkness to obscure the license number, and prayed it worked. We sped off two blocks and I slowed the van down.

We didn't want to draw any more attention than we just had. I got to the train station just as we heard sirens back by the burger shack. Anne had given Megan the crystal and it was just finishing its story to her as we transferred to the new white van. I threw a spell at the old van to obscure any magick, but wasn't sure how good this would be. It was hasty and unprepared.

We pulled out of the station parking lot just as more police cars roared by, lights flashing. We turned left and out onto the street, and drove to Zhirk's truck. We made the final transfer there, and I borrowed another touch of darkness to obscure our magickal signature. Then we drove to Zhirk's house to hide.

Once in the house, I got Anne and Megan to sit in the circle. I told them of the preparations, and to avoid scratching the circle. They sat down and Zhirk turned the television on for them. I got the folder of the General's notes from Zhirk's kitchen, and gave it to Anne, so she could see what we had been given and to reassure her of my and Zhirk's intentions.

The reports of the kidnapping were all over the news, and descriptions of me were being talked about. The girl was a quick thinker there at the burger shack and had used her cell phone to take a picture of our van as it left. She didn't get the plate clearly, thanks to the darkness, but we had apparently been a LOT closer to getting caught than we thought. The police found the van about 5 minutes after we left, according to the news. Maybe exaggeration, maybe not. Having a general's wife and daughter kidnapped, this was news, and the media played it to the hilt. Zhirk had had enough and stomped off into the kitchen to make dinner. He returned and carefully stepped over the circle to give the women a cold sandwich and water.

'Hiding like frightened prey from the hunters. This is fascinating, child. The speed of your heart and the thoughts that race in your mind are delicious.'

I screamed and went straight up. Only through great good fortune did I miss coming down on the circle. Anne and Megan both screamed and huddled in the circle, staring at me with wide eyes.

'Delicious fear, I have never felt it so intensely. It is stimulating. Give me more, daughter of dead parents.'

'You wait until we finish our business, if you please, entity of darkness. Frightening the people I'm trying to protect does not help us finish the contract.' I thought to the voice.

'I will abide for now, but the taste of such unguarded emotions whets my appetite for more and I do grow impatient.' Great, another complication out of nowhere.

The two women were still looking at me, and their fear started to excite me. That was the entity influencing me by its presence. This was shaping up to be a long few days if this kept up. I turned to the two women. "I'm sorry, I got shocked by the lamp when I walked by it."

They looked at me like I'd weirded out. Megan's eyes gazed at me as if planning to challenge the bald-faced lie, but she shrugged and returned to watching the television. Her mother relaxed slowly, shifted to sit next to her daughter, then picked a piece of bread off the plate and nibbled at it. I stepped over the circle and sat down with them.

"Now a little about how this works, I began. "You stay in the circle for as long as you can, but stepping out to go to the bathroom is something you can do. Locator spells take time to work. They are not too precise until you narrow the position of what you're looking for. The longer you're outside the circle, the more feedback the spells will get. So make everything as quick as possible." I thought about what next to say. This is a weird, frightening situation. I just plunged ahead after coming up a zero trying to figure a way to sugar-coat things.

"With you two being the general's family, you can bet whoever is pulling strings on your husband will have powerful casters looking to find you. So stay in the circle. They can't locate you inside it and the darkness screws with the spells so they have to start from scratch if they do get a direction. This should only have to be for a few days, and then we'll get you back home."

"I've got a couple bedrolls for you," Zhirk announced. "I'm sorry I don't have more. Give me a list of things you'd like me to pick up, and I'll go out later to get what I can." He took a deep breath and let it out. "I want to say I'm sorry that things are like this, and you are welcome in my house."

Megan, the daughter, spoke right up on that and her tone could peel paint. "Welcome my ass. We're here because dad wanted us hidden. We didn't have a choice and you wouldn't have us here if you could have found someplace else, pig-breath, so bite me."

Zhirk blinked, I blinked, and so did mom. That was a real slap in the face, but I think I could understand, at least I tried to.

'*Ooh, I like her. Introduce us later human ephemera. She is fascinating.*'

I nearly jumped out of my skin, but to my credit I didn't scream this time. I just hunched over hard and stared at the TV until my heart slowed down again.

The rest of the evening was spent in silence. I think it may have been part of the darkness spell that encouraged that, as even Zhirk and I were unusually quiet throughout the night. No chatting, not one off-the-wall comment or observation. The general's family could have given a stone lessons in being silent.

We turned in very early. I slept in the living room with the girls while Zhirk went to his own bed. I didn't beat him to sleep, and listened to the bone-shaking snores until about two in the morning, by the clock in the kitchen, when he finally rolled on his side and the snoring stopped.

10

T HE NEXT THING I KNEW, it was daylight. The sun streamed
in through the thin curtains, making a bright, warm spot
on the carpet. I blinked the sleep out of my eyes. The two
women were up and eating eggs and cereal that Zhirk had
prepared for them. I went to the bathroom and performed the
necessary ablutions and returned to the circle.

"Why are you with us? asked Anne.

It was a good question. "When Megan's friend took the
picture of the van," I replied, "She may have gotten part of me
in the picture since I was driving. A good mage could use that
to track me, not as easily as you or your daughter, but it does
provide a connection." I paused, and thought about the rest of
the answer.

"You remember how some of the Indian tribes thought
that the camera captured their soul if their picture was taken?"

Anne and Megan nodded. "Well, what the camera did, and the new electronic cameras do also. It's a record of that essence that everyone has. Kind of like Kirilian photography."

I continued after thinking for a bit. "What happens is that you are connected to that picture, and your essence continues to vibrate within the picture. It's you. Which is why we're in the circle. They know you. They have pictures. You're easy to find. Unless you're in here." I tapped the carpet inside the circle.

I took a deep breath. Explaining was giving me some ideas, but I wanted to finish so they knew. Knowledge is power, especially in magick. I empathized with them, they had been clobbered emotionally and they were still holding it together. I admired that, but, somewhere they were going to lose it. I wanted to give them something to think about to delay that reaction as long as possible.

I launched back into the story. "My dad told me that a lot of magick is sympathetic in nature, like if you were real powerful, you could make waves in a bowl and cast a spell that made waves on the ocean. But to get the strong magick, some mages call on the powers for it. Powers are entities of particular aspects of something. I called darkness here as one of its aspects is to hide things."

Megan looked at me. "So you're a what? A Witch? Can you teach that stuff? What can you show me?" There was the gleam of hunger in her eyes as she spoke. She wanted to know. For some reason, her gaze unsettled me, so I answered her question as I tried to shake off the uneasy feeling.

"I'm not a regular practitioner of magick." That was the truth. As far as I know, magick is still being studied and no one knows much about it yet. I mean, the changing was fifty years ago, and that's not a long time to discover a new form of anything. On top of that, a lot of wizards and sorcerers don't like the idea of anyone knowing what they know. Knowledge is power, and the more knowledge you have compared to someone else, the more likely you are to profit. 'Don't share' must be in wizard DNA somewhere.

"So, okay, but when do I get to learn that stuff?" Megan's voice had a whiney edge to it that made me clench my teeth.

"Hush Megan. Anne looked at me, then back to Megan. "I'm sure that if we need magick, Ms. Fatelli will share with us."

Megan looked at her mother. I looked at Megan. She was right on the rebel cusp. Grown up enough to want her own choices, and young enough to have to still look to parents before making one. Megan turned her head and looked at me suddenly. The sensation was like I could feel her looking into me.

I shrugged, trying to be nonchalant. "Look, I can show you a small spell. That's it. If you really want to learn, you do a lot of reading and studying of your own. Calling things like powers will bite you bad. Stay away from them until you know what you're doing."

"Okay." Megan looked at me again, but somehow, I didn't think she meant it.

The second day was a longer version of the first one, with everyone spending as much time as they could in the circle. The television reported that it had received no less than three ransom demands for the return of the general's family. They further reported that the RCMP, the Royal Canadian Mounted Police force for the uninitiated, were doing all they could to identify the kidnappers and their motive. One tip apparently sent them to a seedy hotel near the waterfront. The police blew into the area and locked it down, but all they found was a cheating husband with his mistress. The papers blew that one sky high when it was found that the girlfriend of the mistress had phoned in the tip.

One thing the paper did report was a shakeup going on at Shearwater Air Base. There had been a roundup of several officers and an inventory was ordered into the armaments kept on base. This news had been leaked to the press from an unknown source on the base. So the purge had started, and according to the general, once this started, it would only be a few days and the family could return home. That all shattered an hour later when the news broke that the general had been shot and killed as he left the base to deliver a statement to the police.

Both mom and daughter lost it with the announcement, and they spent the next few hours in a numb sort of limbo. Zhirk and I tiptoed around them. The silence and the situation had gone bad. Really, really bad.

There are, I'm told, four levels of realization to tragedies of this sort. Disbelief, anger, depression, and acceptance. Mom was devastated and grief came to her hard and overwhelming, leaving her catatonic and unresponsive for hours. The daughter was a whole different sort of grief. She stepped into anger after only a few hours and was raging against her dad, me, Zhirk, and anyone that she could name.

Her vocal rage subsided after a while but you could feel the burning anger emanate from her like a roaring fire. This was going to be problematic if she kept it up. I looked over at the mother. Zhirk was helping her up and to the bathroom to clean up. She was coming out of her catatonia, but it would be a while before her grief lessened.

After a quick dinner of hot dogs and french fries, Zhirk and I cleaned up after the two of them and got ready for bed. It was a stressful mix of somber grief and smoldering rage. Megan was wide awake as I settled in the bedroll. I wondered what we were going to do now that the general was dead. Leaving that to tomorrow, I rolled over and went to sleep.

I awoke to a low murmured discussion.

"So you give me the power to hunt my dad's killers, you teach me how to cast spells, and you get to come along for the ride and see everything I do?" asked Megan.

"Exactly, daughter of a dead father. I stay with you and guide you to his killers. I get to experience what you feel," replied a muffled, dark voice.

"Megan!" I said loudly. "What are you doing! No!"

"Deal," she said, and looked smugly at me.

The darkness literally flowed into her. Black ominous smoke enveloped her, making her body indistinct, merging it with the shadows.

Megan stood there, glaring rage and triumph at all of us around her. An aura of menace exuded from her so powerfully, that it had me instinctively shrinking back from her. I looked for the edge of the circle and stepped over it to get further away. She looked at me and her eyes were all black like obsidian. The person that answered was all darkness.

"Our deal will still hold child, but this magnificent creature, and her passion will give me endless opportunity to experience all that humanity has to offer," the Darkness said. "Farewell daughter of dead daughters, we have places to go and people to kill."

I lunged for Megan and was hurled back like a rag doll, hitting the wall and sliding down.

Anne stood up and screamed, "Meggie!"

The entity stopped and I could see the struggle in Megan. She turned to her mother, who said, "Meggie, what have you done?"

"They killed Dad, and I'm going to get them. I'm going to kill them like they killed Dad." Megan sounded like she was dead. Her voice had no emotion, yet I could feel hate rolling off her like a wave crashing on shore.

"Please Meggie!" Anne begged her daughter. "You go out there now they'll know where you are. Your father died to protect you and me. Don't throw away his sacrifice, please. Stay, please, Megan. We've lost your father, don't make me live without you too!"

She broke down at that and started crying, and it wrenched my heart to hear. Megan looked at her mother, and the Darkness answered from her.

"Delicious, this pain. We shall wait and enjoy this, my student of dead instructors. I shall savor this."

Megan sat back down and her eyes returned to normal as the Darkness receded, but the hurt and anger still shone like fire in the night. Zhirk and I retreated to his kitchen to talk. We needed some kind of idea of how to continue with the general being dead.

After about an hour of sitting and trying to come up with a plan, we decided to try and contact the officer leading the investigation the general initiated when he turned on his business partners. Zhirk and I figured it was the best bet to get the mom, daughter, and us, out of this mess alive. Contacting was going to be the hard part. We had to find a way not to get arrested, and not get shot accidentally on purpose by the bad guys that were still loose.

Anne and the daughter were still our responsibility, and I had a reputation to keep. Winning this would definitely be a good boost for my business. Yeah, I know. Mercenary, thinking of the bottom line. Well tough, I have to eat too, just like you. But back to the problem at hand. We couldn't leave the circle, and Zhirk couldn't read anything due to the troll-dyslexia, so traveling somewhere to make a call was out. I had to talk to Fawn.

"Sis, fancy you calling out of the blue." Fawn sounded tired. Which could be good or bad. If she'd put me and the kidnapping together, this could go really bad, really fast. I took a breath and plunged ahead, hoping she hadn't. "Sis, I need some professional advice. Would you come over to Zhirk's after you're off duty?" I asked.

"Sure, Short stuff. See you in three hours." She hung up. Must be a busy day.

We waited, and three hours later on the dot, Fawn knocked on the front door. This was going to be very awkward. I opened the door.

"Fawn, come in, we have to talk."

She took two steps into the room and noticed Anne and Megan. I locked the door behind her as she spun back to me, eyes flashing dangerously. She was all cop at that moment, and I was the perp. It wasn't fun looking at her unspoken accusation. She took a step towards me and glared. Part of me was happy she'd been too busy to run two and two together, another part was wondering why she hadn't.

"What in all the fucking world is going on? You into kidnapping now?" She was as angry as I've ever seen her.

She rounded on Zhirk. "What the goddamned hell are you doing?" she said viciously. "This isn't body guarding. You're supposed to be a solid good guy Zhirk! Ex-fucking-plain this to me right now."

Zhirk gestured towards the file that contained the general's notes. "Read that, and then you can apologize, Fawn. Don't say another word, not one. I'm pissed that you'd even think that I'd pull something illegal. You read that, and then talk to me."

He folded his arms and the anger radiated from him like heat from a fire. It bathed us all and I really hoped Fawn wouldn't get cop-stubborn now. I know they teach cops to stick to their guns with their intent as a way to control the situation and hope to keep it from escalating. But you do not want to get stubborn with a troll, even a small guy like Zhirk. Piss one off bad enough, and people lose limbs, and lives.

Fawn, bless her, knew the score and stalked bad-temperedly over to the coffee table in the circle. She was careful not to break it at this point. Doesn't mean she wasn't thinking it though. I would have been if I was her. It was a very tense fifteen minutes as she read the details in the folder. Both mother and daughter verified the story and showed her the crystal, which activated when they held it again. She looked over at Zhirk, who was still glowering at her. She walked right to him.

"You're right, Zhirk. I'm sorry." She gave him a hug, or tried to.

Zhirk glowered some more, but the hug got him, and he softened. "You're a good cop, Fawn, even when you act like a crazy one, you're a good cop. You're a good friend too."

She released Zhirk and came back over to me. "Sis," she said. "I wish that I didn't have to tell you that the bottle, Hervald, and the bald guy disappeared, but they did, again. I am seriously weirded out by all of this." She shook her head and I think she shuddered. "You keep your eyes open and keep yourselves hidden a bit longer."

"I'll work on ID'ing the good guys from the dirty ones. Then we can move. I'll get people I trust to be the rescue team when we know the score." Fawn turned to the two women sitting in the circle. "I'm sorry for your loss. We'll do our best to get your husband's killer." Anne teared up at that, but managed a "Thank you" to Fawn.

Megan just glared daggers at her. I expected the Darkness to come out, but it apparently had decided to stay hidden for now. Telling Fawn about it would really screw things up, so I kept my mouth shut, and rubbed my temples as her words sunk in.

Great. Zhirk and I were trying to keep two women that persons unknown wanted very much to make dead, and we had to sit in a room with a pissed off teenager that had made some kind of deal with a Power of Darkness that liked to hunt, torture, and kill. This was not something I really wanted to think about. Well, as a friend used to say, "I always sleep on stuff that I can't change; The situation might be different when I wake up." I stepped over the circle and got into my rapidly-becoming-ripe bedroll and took his advice.

I woke up at sunrise the next morning. Zhirk had gone out to get some more groceries. He left a note saying he'd be back around 9am and to make sure that Megan didn't bolt. He'd had to talk to the Power/Megan about staying longer in the circle, and she had agreed to but the entity of Darkness was becoming restive. That was not a good thing.

She leaves the circle, the bad guys will find her and I don't care how powerful the entity is that you have in you, one bullet kills you dead. I didn't want Megan to be on my conscience. I sat down next to her and told her everything I have just explained to you, and while I think she heard me, I couldn't say that I thought she listened.

It's a teenage reaction: you're invincible and nothing can get you until the first time it happens. If the first time is lethal, then there's no more anything. We have all gone through it. Mine was the first time I got mugged. Fawn's was the first time she had to pull her service weapon and use it. It varies for everyone.

Megan, with her anger, and the entity pushing at her, was a bad accident waiting to happen. Short of tying her up, which would guarantee an escape attempt, the only thing I could do was talk. I hoped it was enough.

We stayed in Zhirk's house for another three days with the entity becoming ever more restless and belligerent. Megan was practically bitching non-stop by the third day. It was hard for her mother, while Zhirk and I gritted our collective teeth and tried to keep from gagging her and throwing her in a sleeping bag. But the third day was when Fawn called.

"Be ready, sis," she said, and hung up quickly.

"Okay, Anne, Megan, get your things together. We may be going somewhere else real soon," I said to them.

"It's about time! My stuff reeks and sitting here has sucked big time and I haven't got to see Trey in forever and..."

"Megan, get your things like Ms. Fatelli asked you to," said Anne.

Megan glowered at me and her mother, then slouched over to her one change of clothes and went to the bathroom to change out of Zhirk's shirt. She was back in less than a minute, and threw Zhirk's shirt into his bedroom as she returned to the circle and sat down.

I was going to be very thankful when we finished this job. A change of clothes seemed a wonderful luxury after all this time. Fawn called again two hours later.

"Find a good seedy place and get a room, then you two clear out and leave the ladies there. Watch from somewhere in case the real bad guys get there before us. We'll be in the TAC van. Love you sis, good luck." She again hung up quickly. I looked at the others and said, "We're moving. This is how it goes," and relayed what Fawn had told me.

11

MEGAN WAS EXCITED. Her mom was worried, and was right to be. There was no guarantee that Fawn would get there first, so we would watch the room from Zhirk's pickup. When Fawn showed, we'd get out and let the cops do their job.

We drove over to the 'Laria Inn', which was one of the rent-by-the-hour places where hookers took their customers. We parked, and Zhirk looked the rooms over, choosing the one closest to the street. He stepped ponderously to the door, grasped the small doorknob, then twisted.

The sound of snapping metal was muffled by his huge hand. He pushed the door open and the women went inside. Anne closed the door then leaned something against it to hold is shut. Zhirk and I went back to the pickup and drove through the back part of the lot over to a dry cleaner's. We circled the block to park in front of the motel. The door was clearly visible and we were in position in case the bad guys showed. They didn't disappoint, unfortunately.

One moment was nothing, the next there were five men in street clothes in the parking lot. They clearly had serious magick working. One man going to the front office, the other four to the door. The burliest was carrying one of those big metal persuaders police units use to open locked and bolted bad-guy doors.

I scrambled out of the car and left the door open. Closing it would make noise and I wanted to get as close as we could before things happened. I used a last piece of the borrowed essence from the Darkness and obscured our presence and sounds. It wasn't perfect, but I hoped it was enough to let us get close.

Zhirk had pulled an aluminum baseball bat from the cab and was padding silently beside me a long step to my left. The guy in the office was going to be trouble, but the first job was keep the other four from kidnapping or killing Anne and Megan. We had closed within about forty feet of the four, when one of them stepped back and rammed the 'persuader' into the door, blowing it open. We heard screams as the men poured into the room.

Zhirk and I charged. Zhirk threw his bat overhand like some circus ax-thrower. The bat whistled as it tumbled end-over-end, and embedded in the wall next to the door with a loud crunch. The last man spun and dropped to one knee pulling some small weapon up and aiming at the charging troll. I stopped and raised my revolver, the gunman caught the motion and swung the weapon at me, pulling the trigger as he did so.

Three clods of earth jumped from the dirt immediately to the left of me. I braced like Fawn had told me and aimed for the center of his body. I squeezed the trigger slow and the snub-nosed revolver jumped in my hand. The bullet passed by my target and hit the wall of the motel. Crap! Forgot about civilians! I hoped no one was in that room. The shooter adjusted his target. Zhirk roared, and got everyone's attention in a two block radius.

I was forgotten about as the shooter frantically re-oriented on the now-raging troll and snapped off a burst. It hit Zhirk high in the right shoulder and, if it had been me, probably would have torn my whole arm off. But this was a troll, and he shrugged the impacts off like a horse does flies.

A second three-round burst missed Zhirk, and he grabbed the shooter with a meaty paw. He roared again, then threw him sidearm against the wall of the motel. The shooter hit a window sill with a crunching sound and tinkling glass, spinning sideways to hang limp halfway through the window, with bright red blood leaking down the outside wall.

There were shots and screams inside the room. A second shooter backed frantically out of the motel room, then turned and ran straight into me. We both went fell down in a tangle of arms, legs, and guns. I let go of the revolver, and oriented myself as fast as I could. I was under him with my face in his sternum and his left arm under my right and pushed up towards my head.

I snaked my left arm between our bodies and down to his groin. No padding there. I found that vital organ on the human male, and squeezed and twisted with all the strength I could muster. He gasped and curled slightly and worked his hands toward the center of the pain. I bit down hard as I could on the first piece of flesh that I got hold of and ground my teeth back and forth. He screamed again and my head smacked the pavement hard enough that I lost my grip on his groin. I swallowed a piece of something and rolled to try and get away when his weight lifted off of me. I saw a knee, and kicked at it as I got smacked in the head.

The world spun. I couldn't control any part of me. Through bleary eyes and ringing ears, distant screams and shooting came fuzzily to me. The screaming sounded horrified for some reason, but I was too groggy to understand what was causing the change. I tried to sit up and fell on my side. The screams focused into horrified wails that emanated from Anne and Megan's motel room. I tried to sit up again, and a wave of nausea ripped through me.

I saw Zhirk off to one side reaching for the man that I had fought with. The man was staggering towards the center of the parking lot and reached into his pocket and snapped something between his fingers. He faded from view just as Zhirk lunged for him. He roared in frustration, then spun towards the sounds coming from the motel room. He charged the door, ripping an opening wide enough to let him in. He disappeared into the darkness in the doorway.

One moment later, a roaring, wailing scream of pure terror erupted, drowning out the fading whimpers in the room. Zhirk fell backwards out of the room onto his side, curled up in a fetal position. He covered his face with both hands and cried like a lost child. The other screams in the room had almost faded, but the pure horror in the remaining sounds coming from that black void terrified me. How much worse could it be for the people inside the room?

The screams suddenly picked up in intensity and I heard two shots, a horrified wail of a damned soul, then silence from the room. The darkness faded and I could see inside the room again. Anne came out and fell to her knees near Zhirk and began trying to puke her toes out her mouth. Zhirk was slowly uncoiling, dazed and disoriented by his fear.

I got slowly to my feet, still very dizzy and nauseous. I think I had a concussion. Megan strode awkwardly out of the room, her eyes completely obsidian. Her face was pale as white paper and she was holding herself like she was trying very hard not to puke and scream at the same time.

"You never told me it would be like that!" Megan shrieked, through gritted teeth. "I can't do that! I can't do that again! I can't!" Her head jerked as if she was being forced to listen. She shook her head and said, "No, no, no, no, no," rapidly. She began panting and hyper-ventilating. After a few minutes, her eyes slowly reverted back to normal and she pulled a full breath.

A scream of lost innocence and horror let loose from deep inside her. Megan dropped to her knees and hugged herself harder, and cried, while trembling and rocking back and forth. Her mother crawled over to her and wrapped her arms around her, trying to shield and comfort, and cried with her.

I heard sirens in the distance and staggered slowly over to Zhirk, who was sitting up now, and somewhat alert. I saw the haunted look in his eyes, but ignored it and yelled, "Get up, Fawn's got the TAC team coming and we need to be gone before they get here. Come on!"

Zhirk picked himself up off the ground, dazedly scooped me into his arms, and made a lurching, staggering run back to the pickup. The engine turned over and he pulled away from the curb a few seconds before the TAC van turned the corner and started disgorging police officers. Fawn stepped out of the back and began gesturing. That was the last I saw of her as we turned the corner and drove back to my place.

I went to the bathroom and got some pain killers to help with my pounding head, while Zhirk slumped into a sitting position on his huge bedroll. I swallowed double the recommended dosage and washed them down with water before going to the coffeemaker and turning it on. The smell of brewing coffee deliciously permeated the air. I began to unwind and relax for the first time in days.

I got into the shower and turned it on as hot as I could stand. Just as my muscles started to relax in the delicious heated water, I heard Zhirk. He was crying, like a bass-voiced, heart-broken child. I turned off the shower. Wrapping myself in a towel, I walked quietly out of the bathroom. He was on his mat, still in the same place he had been when he first sat down. He was crying heartbroken tears. "Zhirk, what is it?" I felt like an intruder as I asked.

The grief emanating from him was palpable as he shifted and wrapped both huge arms gently around me. He held me and buried his head in my chest. The sobs came from the pit of his soul. I was flabbergasted, and deeply touched at the same time. This huge mass of muscle bawling his eyes out on my floor like a five-year old.

"I had to see it all again," he mumbled. "I had to watch her die. She screamed for dad and she died slow when they cut her throat. They spit on her and let her bleed out." He took a shuddering phlegm-sodden breath and kept going. "I watched dad die again. I felt him. It was like there was just nothing in him. Oh god I don't wanna be alone like that." The floor shuddered as his body was wracked by sobs.

I just held him as well as I was able. It's not easy being maybe one hundred fifty-five centimeters, forty-eight kilograms of little woman holding three hundred ten kilograms of sobbing troll. It might have been funny under any other circumstance, but here it was right, and the right thing to do. I stood there in that towel for a half hour while Zhirk cried the toxic emotions out of his system.

After he'd calmed down, I went back to my delayed shower and restarted it. After a luxurious half-hour of soaking, I got into some clean clothes and went to check on Zhirk. He was curled up on his side sleeping on the mattress, and I went back to my office and pulled the Murphy bed down and climbed in for a blissful sleep off the floor.

As my luck would have it, I didn't get the nice relaxing sleep I had anticipated, rather I got nightmares of Megan being pulled into a dark place where I could see everything that happened to her, but couldn't hear her. Zhirk was screaming in my voice with Anne. They both looked blankly at me, chanting, "You're the one who did this. He should take you."

I woke drenched in sweat. The clock on the desk said four-thirty in the morning. I was so awake that getting back to sleep for a few hours didn't seem like a good idea. I drew myself a cup of all-night-heated-condensed coffee from my coffeemaker and settled at my desk, wrapped in my blanket, and looked out my authentic dingy 1930's style window. The neon light next to the window blinked on and off, a garish orange against the walls and floor. Sometimes, there's just too much authenticity in my life. That was my last, lazy thought of the night. I don't remember falling asleep.

Zhirk shook me awake the next morning. I yawned and stretched, then got out of my chair to get another long, hot shower and face the new day. After I was dressed, Zhirk went home to clean house and erase the circle. The Darkness I had appealed to had asked to ride within me, only for a short moment, but never had done so to my knowledge. But it did get Megan and was apparently enjoying its ride. Just as apparently, Megan wasn't.

And the bitch of it was, I couldn't change anything. She'd made the deal on her own, without anyone backing her up, and she got in way over her head. The Darkness could ride her for as long as it chose to do so. Her open-ended answer had sealed the deal and now whatever the Darkness wanted to do, it could, using Megan's body as a conduit.

Megan still had control during the day, but the Darkness had it in spades at night. That was bad enough, but to top things off, Zhirk and I had a missing bottle, a missing Hervald, and a missing bald and scary guy probably being maneuvered by magick in some way to cross our paths again. It was enough to make me want to curl up in bed again and shut the day out.

Instead, I got myself another cup of overcooked coffee and went downstairs to the entrance to pick up my mail and a newspaper. Say what you will of the modern internet/world-wide-web and it's probably true. But for me, I like being able to pick up a newspaper and leisurely enjoy reading something that I don't have to stare at using some kind of screen or projection.

I finished a few of the headlines, then stopped to think for a moment. Hervald had been using *Imrits* to watch if anyone was trying to catch him. If the bad guy could do so, why not me? I knew a wizard that could cast the spell for me. With the proper incentives, I could get one or two of the creatures as an extra pair of eyes. The more I thought about it, the more I wished I had done it sooner. An *Imrit* or two is a good investment for the legally paranoid.

12

I WAITED FOR ZHIRK TO GET BACK and then we went over to Potter's Emporium. Lawrence "Larry" Potter is a first-class wizard and almost a better con-man. He didn't really steal from people so much as convince them that a little too much was better than just enough. I'd gotten to know him when he and Fawn were dating in high school. I think he still had a bit of a crush on the Amazon, but he was a funny, generous sort, and a sharp operator. He also got a lot of ribbing because of his name's close resemblance to a series of movies made before the changing.

"Shorty! How are you?" The lean, almost cadaverous look he had jarred almost painfully with the corpulent vision I had of him way back in school. He looked like a modern version of Ichabod Crane, tall and lanky with a protruding Adam's apple and scraggly black hair pulled back into an equally scraggy ponytail. Charms of various sorts and holy symbols of every denomination dripped from his pockets and neck on multiple chains. His jewelry reminded me of the old 'bling-bling' term used by some musicians back in the day. He strode right up to me, and I was enveloped in a long-limbed hug. Zhirk came in through the extra-large front door and looked at Larry. Larry backed up a step and smiled.

"Hey Zhirk, haven't seen you come by for a while. Everything goin' OK?"

Zhirk smiled and said, "Fine so long as you keep your hands off my client." Larry looked at me with a very speculative look.

"Client, eh?" he said. "Well with Zhirky here, you already have enough muscle for six. Hmm, you're here for a little extra protection then? He looked me up and down. "Yes, I'd say extra. But you're not looking for bad-ass magick like most guys. An *Imrit*, right?" he asked with a smile.

"Damn Larry, you still do that to people?" I shook my head at him.

Larry was one of those sorts who had body language down to a fine art. He could look at you and figure out most times what you were looking for and, like with me, sometimes exactly why you came and exactly what you were after. It was like listening to Sherlock Holmes, but without the information on what the deductions were based on. Larry just did it, according to him. It was a great help in his business, and was part of his wizardly reputation on the street.

He motioned to me to follow him into the back of his shop, pausing long enough to ask Zhirk to turn the 'open' sign to 'closed'. He ushered me into a large bare room with a wood floor inset with a large silver circle. Chalk dust puffed up with our steps as Larry bade me sit in a chair in a corner of the room. He then drew an '8' symbol around me and a second chair that he sat near mine. After chalking a six-pointed star inside the silver circle, he drew a smaller circle inside the star. With a big sigh, he sat down on the second chair and meditated quietly for a moment. He began to chant. I settled to wait for a while. Chants, even for *Imrits*, or maybe especially for *Imrits*, are drawn-out affairs. This one came as a surprise though. Larry had barely finished five minutes and an *Imrit* popped into the circle. It looked like a badly drawn rabbit, all angular lines and two long skinny ears that weren't quite the same size.

It chittered and cocked its head quizzically at the two of us. Larry murmured a spell, then chittered back at the creature. He indicated me, and the creature did something that must have been a yes, as then Larry said something loud in that chittering speak, then scratched out a part of the circle. The *Imrit* hop-walked to me and stared at me without blinking. I stared back at it, not sure what to do. I'd never bonded to a creature this way.

"Say 'yes, I accept you' to seal the bargain, Shorty", Larry prompted. "Then you will need to give it a garden of flowers to stay in when it's not with you looking for trouble. You'll also be able to hear it inside your head and understand it somewhat. That'll get easier as you two get used to each other."

"That seemed pretty fast, Larry, getting one like that," I commented as Larry he found a dry-mop and smudged out the chalked circles.

He replied, "Oh it definitely was fast, one of the fastest I've seen." But the fastest was one a few years back. I'd just finished the circle and hadn't even gotten to my chair when the thing popped in. Scared the hello right out of me." He looked at me. "Well, are you going to finish the bargain, or are you going to wait for it to leave?"

I looked again at the creature, and caught its expectant look. "I agree and I accept you." There was a slight trembling in my body and the *Imrit*'s when I spoke the words. *Herd friend?* It was a soft, fuzzy, nose tickling sensation.

"Can you understand me?" I smiled at it, keeping my teeth covered so it didn't think I was trying to eat it.

Yes, came the answer. *You are herd friend, I will help watch for danger, you help watch for food. We share.*

I couldn't put it better if I tried.

You are herd friend, Shorty.

I choked with surprise. "Shorty!?"

Yes, that what herd friend Great Larry name. "Great Larry, huh?" I laughed, eyeing Larry as he was still smudging the circle out. His ears turned red and he had the grace to look a bit embarrassed.

"I figured if I called you Fern, he'd try to nibble you," Larry grinned.

'I be msofchf.'

I started then just shrugged. *Hi Mischief, I'm Fern.* I thought back at him, or her, or it. I had no clue if *Imrits* even had sexes.

With Mischief settled on my shoulder, I thanked Larry, then gathered Zhirk and we drove back to my office to do a little preparation. I was convinced even more by all the things going on that Fawn and I were somehow mixed in with along with magick, which was still trying to find the easiest way through us. Sitting and waiting for Baldy, Hervald, the bottle, or any ugly combination of the above was not what I wanted to do. I wanted to go on the offensive, and change the pattern of this dance.

The first thing would be to get more on Hervald. That was my 'welcome' card into all this weirdness. Some more background might show me something I may have missed. The way to get that was through Fawn.

"I can't give that to you," she retorted.

"Why the heck not, Amazon? You've been giving me tips since you started being a cop, why get all stiff now?" I was glad I was on the phone with her and not in person.

Fawn sighed. "This is different. I gave you tips as help when you were close to stuff that I knew about. I didn't share detailed files on someone's scummy lifestyle or bad habits. Now you're asking for those. I can't help you that way."

"So how CAN you help me then?" I rolled my eyes at the phone and grimaced. This was really getting frustrating. I mean come on, how can you say that giving someone a tip isn't the same as letting them read a file? The information's coming from the same place, just edited. Uh, yeah, the edited part. I grimaced as Zhirk chuckled.

"Okay. Okay. Point for you. Now how about telling me something I could find out without all the information mumbo-jumbo."

"How about this? Go talk to his family and friends and do a little work on the people that were targeted by Hervald and the bottle, before you busted him. Maybe talk with his wife since she was the one that hired you." Fawn was clearly exasperated. "Good God! I have to do all the thinking now?"

I knocked the telephone against the side of my head in frustration. Hervald's wife! She would have all sorts of information on her hubby and his background. This really irritated me, I was being unprofessional, forgetting important things. Time to get smart and get busy. Hervald was a local socialite. Maybe a trip to the newspapers would scrounge something up before I went to see Mrs. Thensome.

"You're right, I should have thought of that angle. Thanks."

Mischief chittered and nuzzled my neck, trying to calm my agitated state. *No danger, herd friend. No danger.* I reached up to rub fingers against its semi-substantial body, trying to rub its neck in the same, reassuring manner.

"Gotcha, Mischief. No trouble here."

"There'll be trouble if you don't hang up and get your ass in gear, gumshoe!" My sister's voice jolted from the phone.

"I got it. Okay. Okay." I hung up the phone, then grabbed the laptop.

"I'm going online, Mischief. You can sleep while I look up some news."

Some digging through online newspapers showed an interesting picture. Hervald apparently married into money when he and Mary Holdwell got together. Mary was seriously nasty old money. Her great-great-grandfather, Hank "The Plank" Holdwell had been one of the biggest cigarette and booze smugglers in Canada back in the 1920's and 1930's.

Mary's grandfather supposedly carried on the family 'tradition', but he was killed when his yacht suffered an explosion just before the changing. Her dad had gone in to the legal system and had made a name as a great Crown Prosecutor for the Maritime Provinces.

Zhirk and I went over to Hervald's place with plans to meet Mrs. Thensome and get a better look at what we were up against. We pulled up in front of a huge two-story house that looked like it had been built in the 1700's. It was square and all red brick from the ground to the roof.

Huge windows dominated the walls, and a strip garden bordered each side of the walk as we approached the door. It was like looking at another time, and I could feel a kind of electricity in the air the moment I started up the walkway. The place was warded to the hilt with protective magicks. Considering her family background, it made sense. Lawyers and smugglers make a lot of enemies.

Mischief started chittering at me. *Predator! Front!* He started to clamber down into my blouse to hide. I yelped and grabbed him. As he wiggled to escape, his eyes rolled wide in fear. I stuffed the *Imrit* into my purse, where it burrowed to the bottom, emitting fearful squeaks.

Zhirk and I stopped at the base of the door steps. Two small lion statues were at the front of the step railings.

"Those look like *Wurmling* nests to me," Zhirk said, and he shrugged deeper into his trench coat. I saw his shotgun shift slightly under the coat to cover the lions.

I looked closer. Sure enough, each one had a *Wurmling* staring alertly out of the lion's mouth. I froze as the two predators focused on myself and Zhirk. Mischief somehow felt their attention, and tried to burrow deeper into the bag. We looked at each other for a few moments. Then, since nothing jumped us, I swallowed dryly, and stepped up to the front door.

My knock brought a large, solidly-built human to the door. He glanced at us through the small window before pulling it slowly open. He looked like those clichés of mobster goons. Almost two meters tall, a meter wide with short black hair and a five o'clock shadow of stubble on his square face. "Can you please state your business here? Understand that no soliciting is allowed on these grounds," he said in a very polite, very flat voice.

"We're not here for solicitations. I'm Fern Fatelli." I stepped forward and put my hand out to shake.

The man in the door eyed it and made no move to be polite. "I will tell Mrs. Thensome you are here. Please wait on the porch." He closed the door.

I spent a few very uncomfortable moments on the porch, watching the *Wurmlings* watch me. They had noticed Mischief and were practically salivating, but they didn't leave the lions. Mischief stayed deep in my purse. Every so often it shivered, bumping my hip. The door re-opened, and a tall, thin woman stood there in blue jeans and a white shirt with a grey sweater on over the shirt.

She cocked her head to one side and the straight brown her swished just like in all those hair commercials. Her brown eyes fixed on my green ones. "Ms. Fatelli? Come in, I'm Mary Thensome. Is the troll with you?" She gestured back out to Zhirk.

I nodded and replied, "Yes, he's my partner, Zhirk."

"Well then, come in please, Mr. Zhirk. Ms. Fatelli and I have a few things to talk about. You make yourself comfortable and I'll get Mr. Rich to bring you something to drink if you're thirsty."

"Thank you ma'am, but I'll be happy with a chair and a television." Mrs. Thensome stabbed at the wall-speaker to inform Mr. Rich of things. She led me back into a small room that had a wooden desk and two laptop computers on it. The desk was set on top of a very expensive looking Turkish rug, with the walls lined with glass-fronted bookcases filled with the thick legal manuals that you'd kind of expect in a lawyer's library.

As I was gazing around, she went over to the large chair behind the desk and sat down, pulled a drawer open, and produced a checkbook. She held it in her hands for a moment. "Would you wish for an electronic transfer or a personal check, Ms. Fatelli?"

"An electronic transfer would be fine, Mrs. Thensome." Faster and somewhat less traceable.

She replaced the checkbook in the desk, and moved to the left laptop. "I'm quite amazed at all that has happened since I hired you," she said as she moused over some screen and clicked and typed. "Without your efforts, my lawyers tell me that Hervald would have had a strong chance at laying claim to part of my family's holdings. But now with all this trouble he is in, they feel that he can be divorced without any loss to my estate."

She finished her typing, clicked her mouse, and then looked at me. "I can't thank you enough. If you don't mind I added a bonus to your fee," she said smiling.

Bonus? "That's fine by me," I replied, "but the main reason I came was to ask some questions about Hervald. With all that's been happening, I'd like to learn a little more about him in case he decides to hold me to blame for your divorce."

She paused for a moment and eyed me.

The *Imrit* whimpered a bit, *She want eat you.*

It's okay, she's wondering how much to tell me, I thought back.

Truly? Mischief thought to me.

True.

"This request is linked to my hiring you?" Mrs. Thensome took a sip from the glass Mr. Rich placed in front of her.

"That, and Hervald's attack on me at my office a few days ago," I said in reply. She blinked in surprise, then quickly regained her composure. "He attacked you? I thought he'd been in a coma. He's awake and loose?" Mr. Rich, grunted in surprise as he stepped into the room.

"Mr. Rich, please tell your partner I'll be wanting him and you for my protection." "I will do so," he rumbled at her, then smiled. The smile vanished as he looked at me. He turned, then walked out the doorway, pulling a cellphone from his pocket. I didn't hear what he said as he pulled the door closed behind him.

Mrs. Thensome looked at the closed door for a moment, then turned to her desk and the laptops. "I have some reports here from other private detectives." She typed and clicked. "I will send a copy of those files to you. Again, Ms. Fatelli, thank you." She rose and shook my hand. "Mr. Rich will escort you and your partner back to the front drive." She returned to her laptops.

Richy boy was waiting outside the door for me, and led me to Zhirk, who was watching a soap opera. He clicked the screen off, then escorted us back to Zhirk's pickup.

13

W E HAD PLANNED to go get Chinese take-out for a quick lunch, but the radio killed that idea. It detailed an attack on a woman who was comatose when she was found. It sounded so much like what Hervald and the bottle had planned for me that I lost my appetite and had Zhirk take me back to my office.

I spent the rest of the day looking over the files Mary Thensome *nee'* Holdwell had sent. It seems that Hervald had been a bit of a con-artist in his early days. There was a trial for false property sales, and one for trying to get money over the internet for foreign children. That all quit after he got caught and sent to prison for twelve years. He got out in three for exemplary behavior and prison overcrowding, according to the detective who submitted the report.

He moved to Canada, somehow passed the bar exam on the first try, and lived a very upscale life as a crown prosecutor, and did quite well for himself. I bet that little change in profession had a lot of money behind it.

He had many steady girlfriends, but the one defining thing about each was a relatively wealthy background. He finally met and married Mary Holdwell, and became a well-known face around town. Hervald also started to develop a reputation as a flirt and that changed last year.

There were apparently numerous women he took up with. Furious with him, his wife had hired detectives to locate a woman who would testify against him so she could get a divorce, but none were able to do so before a mysterious illness rendered them comatose and eventually dead.

Most of these women had been hookers or call girls Hervald used for out-of-town rendezvous, so there were not any real headlines generated. This had been going on for some time then, but when then did the bottle come into his hands, and more importantly, how? It might have been last year when he started having the affairs, but how he got the bottle was a mystery and where he'd go next was a second one.

Zhirk was listening to a radio he had stuck in his trench coat when I checked on him. "What did you find about ol' buddy Hervald there, Fernie?" He chuckled as I sat on the futon next to him. I laid out what I knew as Zhirk listened. Later after I had wound down from the talking, Zhirk said, "So he's been using the bottle to cover up a series of affairs? He must have really wanted to stay married for some reason."

That got me to thinking. Why would he want to stay married so badly? The money in the family? That was the easiest motive to set a theory around. But why do the other women and not the wife? The bottle would have drained her spirit, and he could have inherited the whole estate, if the theory about the bottle's abilities was correct.

Mary Thensome was also somewhat odd. I'd think there'd be a bit more emotion in her from all the stress that usually accompanies a divorce. But what do I know about that? Never been married.

Hervald, if he was being controlled directly by magick, would be going back to the same methods and attacks, and it would be probably ridiculously easy for us to cross our path with his. Magick works that way. Coincidence goes right out the window. It's like a bad novel, *deus ex machina* to the extreme.

The thing Zhirk and I needed to do was find a way to have the meeting at a place and time to our best advantage. The problem was that neither he nor I were sure how to do that. We needed more information, and we need to get a line on Baldy. He was the real wild card. Hervald we had information on, Baldy was a complete blank. To top everything off, we didn't know who really had the bottle. We were guessing Hervald, but it could just as easily be Baldy.

Zhirk had gotten his shotguns out of the pickup and also had his two short-barreled ones out and was inspecting and cleaning them as he sat on his huge futon. He finished the last one with a pull of the cleaning patch and checked the barrel. Reloading all four, he put the two shorties back in the inside rig of the trench coat, and kept the shotguns by the futon within easy reach. "Want him to find us here, or go looking for him?" he questioned.

"How about both?" I replied. "We find ourselves a place that is either remote, or has thick walls and set up there. Make Hervald or Baldy come to us. If we need to start shooting, there's less chance of someone else getting hurt."

"Nice idea, but how can you be sure they'll come looking for us?" Zhirk countered. "Magick or not, I just don't see anyone in their right mind waltzing up to where we are and asking if this is a good time for a shoot-out, or should they come back later when we have bigger guns?" I sighed and made a mental retreat. "So not a good idea. Got any yourself?" I raised an eyebrow at him.

"You still have that piece of cloth?" Zhirk asked. It took about ten minutes to find the scrap of cloth in Zhirk's truck as I had never gathered it up when we found Baldy the first time. Mischief didn't like the idea of looking for a predator, and hated being alone even more, so I had a very unhappy 'herd partner' riding on my lap when we set out to find Baldy again.

We do this why again? To put us where we get eaten? Not good, hide is better.

I sighed and replied mentally. *I don't like it either, but I hate waiting to see when something bad will come find me. I'd rather hunt it myself than be hunted.* Mischief was the least of the distractions though. We'd gotten a slight hit earlier, but lost any trace of Baldy a minute later. Now we had been looking for him for the better part of five hours and no luck.

We go home? The thought skittered across my mind, and startled me out of a light doze. *Yes, Mischief, we go home now*, I thought. I turned to Zhirk, "Let's pack it in, we can try again tomorrow if he doesn't find us first."

"Okay, when we get back let me head upstairs first and make sure we have no surprises waiting." He patted the lining of his trench coat with a smile. *Ever the protector*, I thought.

When we arrived, he was out the truck and up the steps almost before I got out of the cab. A few moments later he came back down, an unhappy look on his face. "Visitors?" I gestured at the windows.

"Visitors", he confirmed, and looked at the old buildings. "They could be in any one of these things watching for us. "Let's not make any bigger targets of ourselves. Get inside."

We went up the steps and locked the door behind us. Mischief went to my desk and curled up on the top while I pulled the Murphy bed down. I heard Zhirk chamber rounds in his weapons. I placed my revolver under the pillow and got to work straightening up all the mess.

The front door had blood on it so whoever the person was, Hervald or Baldy, or someone else, they had been bit by the window. I was betting Hervald as Baldy had used Rynun the time he had ransacked the place. Also this time there was blood on the door, like the person had cut himself. I sponged up the blood with a cloth and set it aside in a plastic bag. I could use the blood for a tracking spell in the morning, one that would give me a good, strong link to the intruder. I was hoping that it would be Hervald, but I really didn't care that much. I just wanted a little revenge for my place being invaded.

To have your personal home broken into not once, but twice in a short number of days is really hard on feeling safe. To put it bluntly, you don't, and I didn't. The cleaning was one way that I could erase everything and feel safer again. It took me about an hour to get the place straightened up, and by then Zhirk was snoring away. I pulled out a book and settled in my desk chair as Mischief crawled over to the bed and flattened out. *You watch for me?*

"Sure Mischief, I'll watch", I said to the *Imrit*. "I'll wake Zhirk up in a few hours and he can watch then for both of us." The *Imrit* sighed and dropped off to sleep immediately. I would love to be able to do that, especially with a troll snoring so loud. I stayed awake until it was Zhirk's turn to get up.

The next morning, we were out and after things by nine. We drove to Larry Potter's, catching him just as he opened. "Hey short stuff, looking to use the back room?" he asked as he unlocked the front door. I kept my mouth closed with sheer willpower, and just nodded. Larry waved us inside and gave me the key to his back room. I spent the next half hour preparing the spell and casting it. Larry's permanent circle helped control the energies and everything went a lot smoother than the casting I did on the scrap of cloth earlier.

When I'd cleaned up, I caught him and Zhirk speaking quietly by the cash register. They both straightened when they heard the door open. "Make sure you watch her, Zhirk, she's a lot headstrong about things. Kinda that small-girl-big-chip-on-shoulder thing."

The spell had a strong pull back over to my part of town and directed us to a building across the street from mine. Zhirk re-checked his shotguns and I made sure my revolver was snug in its holster. I really needed to start thinking about a bigger weapon, and some kind of magickal attack, along with some real protection. This was getting spooky.

The tracking spell led us to the second floor, and as Zhirk was too large to easily fit through the stairwell door, I got to go first and wait until he forced himself through it. He pulled his jacket off, then hunched slightly, wedging himself into the door. The metal and concrete groaned and cracked as he straightened up, then slid into the hallway.

This was one of the taller buildings near Halifax Harbor, just south of the Canadian Forces Halifax base. I closed my eyes and let my other senses wake up. I could feel residual magick powering some kind of ward or warning system as Zhirk finished putting his trench coat on and checking his weapons. The magick had a tinge of death to it, and there was a reason for that. This area had seen a large amount of death many years ago, and certain magickers use that event as an anchor for spells.

This particular building was erected in the 1920's after a huge explosion in the harbor during World War One. The power of the explosion flattened buildings and killed people within a half mile of Pier 6. If that wasn't bad enough, the day afterwards saw the start of a huge, six-day blizzard that killed some of the homeless and severely hampered rescue efforts along the harbor. This building was on the same foundation as the destroyed building, and the sense of old, sudden death lay thick in the air all around the ground floor.

The building exuded a sad, desolate feeling as we walked along the hall. We got to room 604 and that was where the blood trail led us. We got ready. Zhirk brought up one huge foot and booted open the door with the tinkling crash of glass. I ran in and darted to my right as soon as I got past the doorway.

PREDATOR! Mischief screamed in my head and dove off me to the right. I followed, landing awkwardly, off-balance as adrenalin charged my senses from Mischief's scream.

Something crashed into the wall above me, and I saw a *Wurmling* lock onto the wall and bore through like a hot knife through warm butter. I rolled and got my pistol clear of its holster. Hervald had two of the creatures.

The second one drew a bead on Mischief as it skittered through the inner doorway. It hunched and arrowed straight at the *Imrit*, which neatly slid to the left and the *Wurmling* hit the wall, with the same result. Zhirk's shotgun bellowed in the hallway.

I heard a second shot, and hoped he had killed the thing. I looked for where the other one would be coming. It was too stupid, I hoped, to bore back through the wall, so I covered the inner doorway and braced prone for a shot. Sure enough it came round the corner. My first shot missed and the creature ducked sideways and crouched at me.

I aimed and slowly squeezed the trigger like Fawn had told me, and the bullet kicked up plaster in its face. It skipped backwards in surprise from the near miss and reset to leap, when a loud boom slapped me on the side, and a burst of silver buckshot hammered the *Wurmling* into paste.

I turned my head and saw, rather than heard, Zhirk chamber another round. The *Imrit* gibbered in fear and huddled in the corner as Zhirk helped me to my feet. "Got them both, but damn they're fast. Missed the little leech with the first shot," he said in a whisper as he reloaded the shotgun.

We both sat very still and listened with what hearing we had for any movement in the other room. *Mischief, can you peek fast into that room? Is the man in there waiting for us?* I asked the *Imrit*.

I scared herd friend, I scared! it mentally replied.

I need you to be brave herd friend. Can you look around the corner and see the predator? Please, it is very important, I appealed to Mischief.

The *Imrit* quivered and slowly moved to the corner of the doorway. It peeked around the corner, then darted back to me. The full mental picture of what it had seen gave me a chill. Hervald was there, on the floor braced and covering the door with a pistol of some kind. He was in the corner along the wall, the door was open. His position gave us an option besides going through the door into blazing gunfire. I whispered to Zhirk and pointed along our shared wall where I thought Hervald would be.

Zhirk slowly stepped back and motioned me back towards the outer doorway. He shrugged off his trench coat, and handed it and the weapons to me. A few deep breaths and he lowered his shoulder and charged the wall. He hit it like a wrecking ball and burst through to the other side. There was a yelp of surprise and three quick shots. Zhirk roared in rage and pain, there was a scream, a thud, a snap, and quiet.

I stepped through the hole, and saw Hervald in a heap against the far wall. Zhirk was bleeding from two holes in his left leg where the bullets hit. I looked at Hervald and saw that his left leg was folding the wrong way ninety degrees to the left of where it should be pointing. I looked at the amenities, trying to find something to staunch the blood coming from the bullet holes. All that was available was a blanket, two flashlights, a crowbar, and Hervald's gun.

Zhirk grabbed the blanket and commenced tearing it into thin strips to wrap the bullet wounds with, while I went over to check on Hervald. He had a pulse and I figured he should be fine for the time being. I wasn't going to waste time on him, and went over to help Zhirk finish wrapping the wounds.

Hervald actually was awake when I went back to check on him. His eyes were open and drool fell from his lips, just like the last time I saw him on the floor. The lights were on but no one was home. This was getting too weird for my taste.

How the hell could a shell like this actually operate, much less operate intelligently? The answer hit me. Remote control. Someone was either programming Hervald's body or using it. I thought about it some more and was convinced that someone was using it like a set of clothes. Hervald's soul had gone somewhere and this shell was being used by someone else. How else could this body pull the trigger of a pistol or think to lay prone to minimize a target?

I hit the speed-dial on my beat-up cell phone. "Zhirk, can you find something to tie Hervy up with? I'm going to call Fawn." She wouldn't be overjoyed to get Hervald back, but she'd be happy to try and keep him in jail this time.

Two escapes in a month by the same person can really make a police department cranky. They'd be very tight on Hervald so there'd be no third escape. Baldy and the bottle were two other complications I had at the moment. Much more worrisome ones also. I didn't have a troll tying them up.

That was very brave of you Mischief, thank you. We stopped the bad predator. I communicated to the *Imrit* who was still back at the doorway watching everything with wide eyes.

It is harmless? I did good! It swelled slightly and ambulated awkwardly to me, pressing itself against my leg. *We did good, herd sister, 'we'.* Mischief broadcast back to me, and I felt the warmth of its presence against my leg. Simple trust can do a lot for your feelings.

Zhirk finished using Hervald's belt to loop his hands and feet together, while Fawn listened as I told her where to come and get Hervald. She had the same thought I did, and had already requested a police car detailed exclusively to cruise the area I lived. The car pulled up outside in under thirty seconds, and the two officers were up with us in under a minute. They hauled the trussed up escape artist back to police headquarters after taking quick statements from Zhirk and me.

We were down one, at least for a short while. Baldy and that bottle were still out there somewhere, and, considering things, I had the feeling we'd cross them soon enough. I still had the scrap of cloth, and that would still locate its last wearer if we got close enough, but its usefulness was waning. Keep something away from the imprinted source too long and it slowly returns to a neutral state. We were coming up against that time limit. I could feel my spell fading.

Zhirk and I went back to my office. Once there, we settled down to think some of this over and rest. I had missed two clients in taking the one job involving Anne and Megan, so I was at loose ends. Clients were needed. They're how I make my living, remember? That, and I really hated waiting for Baldy to make an appearance to attack me again. That got me thinking.

Okay, so what might make me so interesting to magick? There had to be an answer, but it was also such a reach for an answer. Plus it was one with a lot of hubris. Why would magick be interested in twin sisters? What was the reason? Magick may use the easiest course to fulfill its requirements, and it doesn't have to be logical. However, like a stream going downhill, there is a reason why magick flows where it does.

In the case of a stream, the ground might be lower in one spot, or softer, and more easily carried away to reinforce the channel. Magick, like I explained at some length earlier, works in the same manner. If I was right, somehow Fawn and I were the easiest 'channel' for magick. The trouble with this thought is that for the life of me I couldn't figure out why it would be that way.

Dad and Mom were the wizards. Fawn and I gave that up when they died. We had a decent smattering of learning it like most kids did these days. But neither of us were particularly gifted in its use. Potential? No more than the average practitioner. Mom and Dad were supposedly exceptionally powerful and practiced. Maybe Mom and Dad were the answer then. I had to talk to Uncle Todd and see what he knew about my parents that I didn't know.

14

Zhirk and I pulled up at Uncle Todd's place in Cole Harbor. It was a small bungalow nestled among near-identical bungalows that had been base housing at one time. Uncle Todd's was a quiet tan in color, and the porch dipped slightly at the front due to settling. The place was tidy, and the small garden in the front of the house gave it a cheery look, one that I remembered well from living here up until about ten years ago, when I turned eighteen and left.

Fawn stayed another two years, and moved out after Aunt Ruthie had died. Uncle Todd had lived here alone since then. I walked up the familiar steps and he was at the door before I even had a chance to knock.

"Fernie! Com'ere and give your Uncle Toddie a hug," he said as he swept me into his arms. Uncle Todd was a rail. He was near one-point-eight meters tall, but ridiculously only around sixty-five kilograms. His lean face reminded me of the anteaters at the zoo. He had a thick shock of black hair, and a thick, greying mustache. He had on old, comfortable khaki pants and a denim shirt of faded brown. Bright red suspenders clipped on the baggy khakis, a bright splash of color over the soft earth tones.

As always, Todd was happy to see me. He was one of those people with open arms for anyone who came by. A genuine 'treat everyone as you want to be treated' person, who actually lived the words. True to form, he stepped off the front porch and greeted Zhirk like a long-lost friend who just happened to show up. We entered the house and sat down, me on the old recliner and Zhirk on the floor as there was no furniture big or sturdy enough for him.

Todd looked at our faces and picked up on the mood. He went into the small kitchen, and a moment later, brought us some lemonade. As he settled on the sofa next me, he said "This isn't just a social call, is it? Your friend there," he nodded at Zhirk, "has a shotgun. What's got you spooked?"

"I need to know more about Mom and Dad, Uncle Todd. I have someone after me and there's weird stuff that's happening. I got a bottle that seems to drain a person. I got weird magickal stuff going on. I got a guy that's a drooling vegetable, that's like a puppet on someone's string. And there's a guy that's seriously powerful, and can leap a three story building. That's what's going on." I leaned against Uncle Todd, inhaling the soft pine scent of his aftershave.

"You're the only one that knows what Mom and Dad were doing when they died, and I need to know, Uncle Todd. It's weird, but I believe that it's all tied together by Mom and Dad. Please, can you tell me more about them?"

I watched him sit back up and swallow. After a long sigh, he replied, "All right, you're old enough. But do you mind me calling Fawn here to join us? I want to tell you, and I really don't want to tell the story twice. Once is going to be hard enough," he finished, with a wistful, desolate look. He got up from the sofa, then walked back to the kitchen, and the only phone in the house.

About fifteen minutes later, Fawn strode grimly into the house. Uncle Todd smiled sadly and gave her a big hug. She closed her eyes and returned the hug, her chin resting on top of his shoulder. Uncle Todd stepped back, and collapsed onto the sofa, uncomfortably rigid as he waited for Fawn to sit down. She flashed me a flat smile as she sat on the arm of the sofa next to me, then looked over at Uncle Todd. I looked at him with her. Uncle Todd really looked like he wanted to forget the whole thing. His body was piano-wire taut, and you could feel the reluctance vibrating in the air. He took a deep breath, then began.

"First off, you got to understand that this was still when the changing was new to everyone. You had all sorts of people trying to practice magick the way they thought it should be done. A lot of those people were lonely, desperate, or just plain nuts. Most of the world didn't think about magick. Magick that worked was pretty hit and miss. The effects were uncontrolled and intense. Mike and Cathy were two of the few who enjoyed a stable belief in magick. They saw it as a natural part of the world, and enjoyed the quiet communing with nature that the Wiccan religion provided."

Todd sighed and looked away as if he were seeing the story. "They'd been married eight years before the changing and wanted children. Whatever the reason, despite all their efforts and all those of modern science, Cathy never was able to get pregnant. When magick came back into the world, they, like a lot of the others, were caught unawares. Fortunately, their first accidental spell didn't kill them. They worked together carefully after that, and quickly learned methods and rules that helped them survive learning magick. They eventually garnered enough magickal control to attempt to have children. Fawn, you and Fern are the result of that. Twin girls. They were ecstatic to have the two of you and were very happy for five years. But that sixth year, we had a plague sweep through Halifax, and you two got very sick."

Fawn and I shifted in our seat. Zhirk remained a quiet lump on the floor. He'd closed his eyes, his whole being absorbed with listening. Uncle Todd closed his own eyes for a minute, then opened them, and continued. His voice started to get hoarse. Whatever he was going to say, he really didn't like.

"Your parents were desperate. The plague was one of those that had developed immunity to modern antibiotics. The two of you were going to die. Your dad called me and asked me to stand in on a ritual to try and save the two of you. Our casting was a dismal failure. The spells were not strong enough to fight the disease. Your mom got the idea to cast a different kind of spell. This one was an invocation to the other side of the life force, death. Cathy came up with the thought to barter a life for the two of yours. She convinced your dad it was the only way to save you two. So they worked a calling and attracted an entity of pure malevolence."

I looked at Fawn who was wide-eyed. I think I was as well. Mom had called to Death to save us. Uncle Todd had tears rolling down his face. His features stilled as he exerted his will.

"They called it Semjaza. I think it was some kind of demon or avatar. They bargained for its assistance, and it agreed. Semjaza gave them the method to create and cast the spell to save your lives. Your dad had reservations, but like any parent, was willing to go to the extreme to save his children. They researched the spell for three days, and then fasted for two more, making sure that they were in harmony with the world around them before casting the spell."

Uncle Todd stopped and looked at us. His eyes were haunted as he thought about how to say it. "The first part of the spell went without difficulty. It was the second part where things got tricky. Your parents were so deeply into the natural part of the world, and to call something so unnatural upset a lot of things in and about them. They were committing a rape of life energy, drawing it off from the plants and animals around them, feeding it to Semjaza in exchange for your two lives."

His voice cracked as he returned to the story. "I messed the spell up. You girls started screaming and collapsed as the magick began to flow into you. I saw pieces of you flaking and floating away to that thing your parents called up. Your dad saw what was happening and tried to abort the spell. The power had control by then. He and your mother were locked into the casting. When Mike stopped chanting his part of the spell, it began to collapse." Uncle Todd looked bleak. It was like the color had gone out of him, and his clothing. It all felt like, I don't know. Words can't describe the sense of loss, of desolation, that I got from looking at him.

"I wasn't as direct a part of the spell as you four were, and when Mike and Cathy started screaming, I froze. Your dad started chanting again, and yelled at me to save you two by completing the spell. Instead, I pulled you both from the circle and ran to the cars. You two were screaming like damned souls, that thing was howling in rage about something, I don't remember what."

We all paused to take breaths. Todd went on with the story. "I looked back and saw a swarm of black blobs emerge from the its mouth and float over to your parents. Wherever they touched, a gouge of flesh disappeared and blood spurted, and the blob returned to that demon. I didn't watch any more, you two were screaming. The flaking had stopped, but something flowed back into the two of you when I pulled you off the pentagram. It was like a greasy smoke that emanated from your folks and the demon. It cut off when you were in the car." His haunted look made him seem even thinner, gaunt like a starving man.

"I ran to the driver's door and yanked it open. Your folks started screaming for me and I looked back. They had large pieces missing and Semjaza was screaming at them still." Tears were streaming down Todd's face as he forced himself to finish the narrative.

"Your mom looked right at me and I could see her pleading for me to come rescue her. Your dad was screaming in utter terror as those blobs took pieces of him. The ground was wet with blood." Todd's rate of speech quickened. "I panicked and drove like all hell was chasing me. When I got you two home, you were both unconscious. All I could think of was to put you in bed and talk with Ruth."

"The next morning, when we checked on you, you were both like puppets. Eyes open and just lying in bed. No reaction to anything. Later that day, I noticed little wisps of something floating around the house. It seemed thickest near your door. I looked in and saw faint black smoke flowing into you. The black stuff was from the spell I guessed, so whatever happened was still going on."

"Ruthie and I set up a quick circle. We weren't as near as practiced, nor as powerful as your folks. The spell took all day and most of the night, but we managed to cast a spell that cut the link to whatever it was. You girls woke up the next morning like nothing ever happened, and we just carried on. You didn't seem to remember what happened that night. You never really asked about your folks, and we just went along with that. Ruthie figured you'd ask eventually." Uncle Todd drew a shaking breath.

"The hard part was listening to you scream on the anniversary of the casting. It'd happen right at the time the spell started, and stop at the time we blocked the spell from you. I don't know why. I don't know how. It just happened."

"Other than that, you were normal, healthy kids. In fact, you never did get sick from anything again after that night. For that matter, now that I've thought about it, neither have I." He took a deep breath, and looked at me and Fawn. "That's the story. You now know as much as I remember. I hope it helps." He stood up, looking at Fawn and I. "Now you know, and lord knows, I want to forget it all." Uncle Todd shuffled tiredly into his bedroom and locked the door.

No one moved at all. I could hear Uncle Todd crying behind the door. I'm sure Fawn and Zhirk heard it too. We got up as silently as we could, and quietly left the house, which seemed changed after the story. Everything had a kind of loss to it, as if nothing was whole or would be again. Fawn surprised me, giving me a quick hug. She ran to her car, got in, and drove off without glancing back.

Zhirk and I got into his truck, and rode all the way back to the office in silence. I don't know that the story helped at all. It was confusing to me. We were going to die and they used 'black' magick to heal me and Fawn. Then my parents were eaten by something because they didn't finish the spell. Uncle Todd and Aunt Ruthie blocked the spell somehow, so it didn't keep putting something into us? That's what it sounded like to me.

I wanted to talk to Fawn in the worst way, but she had turned off her cell phone. I called her desk and Detective Marin answered and let me know that she had called in sick. Fawn would need a lot of alone time for this apparently. We knew something had gone wrong, but this was really opening old wounds we didn't know we had in each of us. Still, with Baldy being out there and stuff swirling around magick-wise, she'd be smarter to be with someone so they could cover her back.

I didn't know where to look so I borrowed a line from Uncle Todd talking about what his granddad told him about some place called Viet Nam - 'If you're stuck and can't do anything about a situation, get some sleep. It may have changed when you wake up'.

15

I WOKE UP THE NEXT MORNING when Zhirk shook the Murphy bed gently. Gently meaning I didn't fall on the floor. "How ya feelin' after all that story?" he asked as I grumpily tossed my pillow at him.

"Bite me. I feel like I haven't even slept yet," I replied and rolled out of bed and shooed him out of the room so I could change clothes. After cleaning up and flipping the Murphy bed, I went out to see Zhirk, who was gathering his clothes and stuffing them into a pillow case so he could wash them.

"What's next today?" Zhirk questioned as he finished his domestic chore.

"Look for Baldy and see if we can find out about that bottle somehow," I replied. I didn't see how that story of Uncle Todd's fit yet, but the feeling was there that it was part of things. I hoped that I wasn't on some wild chase after my own tail. We went over this time to the 'Magick Cornucopia'. The apothecary that we had tracked Baldy to earlier.

The store had just opened and the proprietor was turning the sign in the front window from 'closed' to 'open' as we pulled up. We received a cheery wave as we exited the pickup and a warm 'hello' as we entered the store.

The owner of the shop, Elvira Crabtree, her real name, I swear to god, was a plump, square woman of anywhere from mid-forties to early sixties. Her brown-gold hair was loose and straight, hung just brushing her shoulders, with just a few traces of gray beginning to show. The shop had a warm spicy smell, like pumpkin pies fresh from the oven.

The whole store seemed to exude that kind of comfort and peace. Elvira's voice intruded on my thoughts and brought me back to the business at hand. Baldy. I smiled at her and said, "Ma'am, do you remember the incident a few days ago, when your sign was wrecked? Do you remember the man?"

"Why yes, I do. He asked if I could order some items and ingredients for him. But the items were fairly exotic, and I wasn't able to help him," she answered. Her eyes flicked over me, taking in the brown slacks, ivory shirt, black suspenders, and my tan snap-brim fedora. She didn't seem to disapprove, so I jumped into the nitty-gritty.

"I know this is unusual and that you understand I'm not a cop, but I would like to know what he was after. I'm investigating him and am trying to put pieces together." I gave her what I hoped was a reassuring, and slightly pleading half smile. She looked at me, suddenly very alert, and not at all the cheery proprietor of a moment ago, "I remember a few of the things he was after. Why do you want to know?"

I mentally started to construct an answer, but the place actually felt like it was so safe that the truth wanted to come out. I closed my eyes and opened my other senses. A subtle magick was at work here making me want to trust people. I caught myself. Oh she was sneaky. Not powerful, but very skilled at what she knew. So I nodded, then made a show of thinking. "He has an interest in me, so I felt that I ought to know more about him."

"I see," she said. "Well, tit-for-tat, I understand that. He was after a mandrake root, bladderwort, Psilocybe Cubensis powder - 'magick mushrooms' to you." She tapped her temple with her ring finger as her face scrunched up. "That, and something else, I don't remember what. Oh! Oh yes. He was looking for a florist who specialized in exotic plants."

"Did he say what kind of plant he was looking for?" I wrote down the ingredients.

She paused, and again looked me over very carefully. She shrugged, then replied, "No, just that he wanted to find such a dealer here in Halifax. I told him about Moore's Greenhouse on North Burns. Then he called and asked for something tri-colored."

"Thank you. I appreciate your help," I said to her as we left the shop.

She gave us a cheery wave. "Come back anytime."

We arrived at Moore's Greenhouse and were met as we entered by a short, thin man who introduced himself as Milford Green, the proprietor.

"What can I help you with friends?"

Before we could answer him he started talking again. Apparently the pause was just him wanting a good breath to talk some more. "I have all the items you need to work a garden or help build a landscape business. I am, in fact, the major supplier for a number of the landscapers here in Halifax and Dartmouth," he told us rather pompously.

I did have to agree he had much to be proud of. The greenhouse was huge and just one of four on the property.

Each greenhouse, he told us with a smug smile, was dedicated to a different continent and their plants. He looked like he was about to launch into another self-important description of his business, so I jumped ahead with a quick question of my own.

"I was wondering if you remember a call about a week and a half ago. It was for umm, something tricolored, I think," I said, watching closely for his reaction.

He was irked I'd interrupted him but as the question sunk in, he became lost in thought for a few moments, then came alert and snapped his fingers. "Right, I remember, Ipomoea tricolor, it's a Morning Glory variety. A man called up about that time and asked if I had any of that plant for sale," he said and then continued as he warmed to the subject.

"It's one of the night-blooming plants and the seeds are mildly hallucinogenic. The Aztecs were said to have chewed the seeds before some of their ceremonies. The gentleman was wanting to order a couple of the plants. I didn't have any but placed an order for him that came in two days ago." He looked at us both. Zhirk grinned, and I could see the man visualizing a rampaging troll in his greenhouse. The image was so clear on his face both Zhirk and I nearly lost it.

"You here to pick them up?" he inquired in a voice that only squeaked a little.

"No," I said to him, fighting the urge to break into giggles. "What we were hoping to do is see if you had any more information about him. We're not police. I'm a private investigator and I'm trying to get background on him where I can find it."

He looked us over, the relief palpable. We could see him concentrate. His eyes lit up and turned to us with all the smoothness of a used car salesman. "Tell you what, you buy those two plants off of me, and I'll see what I can find in my records."

We agreed. It was a relief in a way. Any more of his antics, Zhirk and I both would have blown the deal with laughter. He mumbled to himself as we finished the transaction. "I must be crazy. Why else would I do it? Don't make sense, but it feels right. Lords above, I hope I ain't goin' crazy." He finished writing up the sale, and we had two new plants for the office. He then went back to see if there was anything in his transactions or records. A minute or so later, he returned, waving a slip in his hand.

"Got something for you. A guy named Hervald Thensome ordered the exact same flowers a day ago, and requested them delivered to this address." He handed me the slip, which I memorized, then handed back to the florist. Zhirk thanked the man, then we hurried back to the truck and drove to the address.

The address took us to a location that turned out to be a dilapidated house in a dilapidated part of town. The brown paint was peeling off the neglected wood. Plywood covered some of the broken windows. All the aforementioned windows had rusted metal bars to keep outsiders from breaking in. Though there were no vehicles around the house or nearby in the street, we knew that didn't guarantee an empty house.

People in the area were eyeing us speculatively as we stopped. The speculation turned quickly to minding their own business when Zhirk got out of the truck. No one wanted a piece of something like Zhirk. No one smart, that is.

We approached the front door. Zhirk took the door knob in his great hand, and twisted. The slight squeal of shearing metal came to my ears. The bolt failed with a faint, metallic 'pop'. It was only just a slight bit tougher for Zhirk to get leverage enough to tear through the dead bolts. It constantly amazes me that people spend money on something like a dead bolt and then mount it on a piece of thin wood. We entered the house.

Not surprisingly, the inside was much like the outside. The sheet rock showed a lot of water damage, and in places sagged and bulged like the wall itself was in the last stages of a pregnancy. Spots of paint speckled the walls, with the majority fallen to the floor. The dingy living room led to a small kitchen that reeked of damp mold and rotting wood. Zhirk wrinkled his nose and sneezed. My gag reflex almost got the better of me. Whoever lived here had to have an iron constitution, and no sense of smell or personal hygiene. Mischief whiffled irritably at the smell and burrowed as deep as it could into my coat pocket.

Zhirk tapped me on the shoulder and pointed at something in the back room. I went back there and we found a five-pointed star on the floor. Three points had items on them. One point had what looked like Psilocybe Cubensis powder, another had one of those Impona flowers on it, and a third had a wet weed of some kind on it. I looked more closely at the weed. Bladderwort. I'd seen it in the stagnant ponds and marsh outside of town when Fawn and I were growing up.

The last two points were empty. It had me wondering what items four and five were going to be. I couldn't make any guess of what the three ingredients represented. "Fernie, this one isn't ready for casting, is it?" I glanced back at Zhirk. "Nope, which means we know where he's got to come back to. Let's look around some more. Maybe there's something that'll give us an idea about what the casting circle is for." *I no like this, predator live here. Bad predator. Smell bad.* I concurred and patted the pocket Mischief was in.

In the corner of the room on a wooden stool was the shiny metallic glass bottle that Hervald had when he attacked me the first time. We had two choices. Leave it, and hope that Baldy didn't plan to use it, or pocket it, and use it as a tracer back to the owner. As you say, a no-brainer. We'd already left way too many things disturbed. I pocketed the bottle, took the items, and did my best to memorize the circle. I wanted to be able to set it up back at the office so I could puzzle out what Baldy was trying to do. Then I smeared it. I broke each line, disfigured every symbol. I don't know about you, but leaving something like that casting circle ready to be used just didn't seem like a good idea to me.

We searched the rest of the rotting house, and didn't find anything else we could link to the circle or Baldy. There was no trace of Baldy beyond the spell circle. I looked at Zhirk. "Can you think of anything we missed?" He just shrugged his massive shoulders, clearly disgusted with being here. We left and got in the truck. As the pickup started and backed into the street, there was a howl of outrage that came from in the house. Baldy burst out the front door running right at us.

"How the hell did we miss him!? I screamed.

Mischief wailed from the pocket, and tried to press against my body. *PREDATOR!*

"Ya think?!" I screamed back as Zhirk slammed on the brakes. The tires shrieked as the pickup, slowed and spun sideways, so the driver side was to Baldy. At that moment, I think both Zhirk and I had the same thought; if we caught him now, we'd be taking care of a lot of our problems.

Baldy gave us a different solution. He ripped away one of the posts holding the roof over the porch, hefted it without effort and threw it like a spear at the pickup. The only reason it didn't kill us outright was that his aim was off and it punched through the wall of the bed just in back of the cab, and out the other wall like a laser beam and bounced in the street some thirty yards downrange. By the sheerest stroke of luck, it managed to miss the gas tank as well, but don't ask me how. Zhirk yelled something I didn't quite hear, I was too busy yelling, "Shit! Drive! Go! GO! GO!!"

Zhirk floored the gas pedal and we fishtailed away from Baldy who moved to the other column and ripped it up and threw it at us. The odd side-to-side motion of the fishtailing truck saved us from getting another big hole in the cab as it just missed on my side and carried away the side rear-view mirror. Baldy started to run after us but, for some reason, didn't have the amazing speed or agility he had earlier. We built up speed and soon left him behind, still screaming incoherently at us.

"Gods and outsiders," Zhirk exclaimed heatedly. "How did he get so strong?"

"I don't know, but I don't think we want to try capturing him alone," I responded. "I'm not sure we could do it without killing him."

"Killing Him?! Did you SEE what he just did to my truck!?" Zhirk took a shaky breath. He skin was a couple of shades paler than normal. "The last time I ever saw something that strong was… never, come to think of it. This is just plain scary."

I agreed completely with him. Baldy had taken the stakes to a completely different level. I mean, I looked at him and was ready to pee my panties, he scared me so badly back there. As we calmed down and drove towards Zhirk's place, I tried to think about what to do.

If I called my sister again and explained about Baldy, she would be after him and probably find him. What happens then? My imagination conjured up an enraged Baldy attacking the whole TAC unit and ripping them limb from limb like some people pull legs off flies. My sister would try to go against him like that and die, horribly.

We go home! We go hide! Mischief was beside itself with terror after the encounter, repeating itself over and over. I agreed with him but hiding wouldn't solve anything, and it might get someone I knew hurt. The problem was we just didn't know enough.

So how could we stop Baldy? Magick held one answer, but it was something that had to be set up and done ahead of time. Casting spells in the middle of a fight or some other activity was not something I could do. I could set a binding circle, but I had to get Baldy into the circle for it to work. That meant luring him to the location.

Or, alternatively, letting him get a fix on the bottle and use it to trap him. The bottle! Insight lit my mind up. The bottle was something Baldy apparently set a great store by. So letting it lead him here seemed like a good idea. But we had to really get the circle set correctly. That got me to thinking about the items Baldy had been trying to get his hands on.

Mandrake root was used for sympathetic magick when you wanted to affect some person. Magick mushroom powder was a strong hallucinogenic, and maybe a spiritual focus. The night-blooming plants were for something, maybe some kind of night-specific ritual. The seeds were supposedly hallucinogenic also. But bladderwort? Why would someone use Bladderwort? It's not even an herb, just a weed as far as I understood it.

"Zhirk, what do you know about Bladderwort?"

"What's a Bladderwort?"

I grimaced at his lack of helpfulness. I had some hunting to do and, fortunately, the internet has lots of information just waiting to be accessed. I found my answer quickly. Bladderwort is actually a carnivorous plant. It lives in swamps and bogs where water is acidic, and nutrients are low. Its method of capture is in the small chambers, or bladders, on the plant that are under water. The bladders act as a suction trap. A creature hits one of the trigger hairs on the bladder, and a small trap door opens and the walls expand, sucking the creature into the trap. The door closes and the creature is trapped inside. Excess water is removed and acids dissolve the captured prey. In fact, you could kind of say it was a natural bottle, which made sense then. It was a component that was to represent the bottle in some spell, or a function of the bottle. That was my best guess with what we knew.

There were five components to the spell. We knew that from the casting circle back in the house. The plant went on one point, the Psilocybe Cubensis powder on another, the bladderwort on the third, and the mandrake root on the fourth, but what went on the fifth point? The bottle? Not likely as the other parts were plants, and natural. The bottle wasn't and that would mess the casting. It had to be something natural then. Maybe another plant?

As I settled down to get some sleep, Zhirk finished cleaning and re-loading his shotguns. The metallic *clack-clack* of the slide action was loud, and comforting, in the quiet room. Baldy was out there, and one of us would always be awake. I took my shift after two a.m. Zhirk handed me his shotgun, then settled on the bed, and was asleep instantly, his thunderous snores vibrating the floor and making the small knick-knacks dance on their shelves. I got him up at nine, and we thanked God for a quiet night. We both had been expecting an immediate visit from Baldy, and to have it not happen was relieving and stressful at the same time.

I spent the rest of the morning building the casting circle as well as I could from memory, and put the four ingredients on the points, while trying to get a feel for that fifth ingredient. Trouble is, it could be anything. Time to go get an expert. I called Larry Potter again, and asked him to come over.

Larry knocked 'shave and a haircut' on the front door. Opening the curtain, I saw his lean self on the landing. He looked over at me. I waved to him from the window and moved to open the door. "You know, seeing you two is becoming a habit," he said with a wide smile. His long strides carried him to the center of the room.

"You just love the attention," I replied and returned the smile. Larry was a good guy, and a steadfast friend. Maybe I ought to see a little more of him after things quieted down. I led Larry back to the casting circle. We'd had to move Zhirk's futon to make room and the office was just big enough for the circle.

"So what are you wanting called up now? Another *Imrit* to keep yours company? Or something else?" His attention centered on the circle. He took a couple of strides to his left around the perimeter, his eyes taking everything in. "I'm trying to identify what kind of circle this is supposed to be and what the missing ingredient is for it," I replied, as he stared at the circle.

"These are the ingredients that you know, hmm, mushroom, what kind of flower is that?" he asked. I told him what I found out about it. "Mandrake and, bladderwort, you said? Hmm, psychedelic, spiritual, night, trap? Man, quite the puzzle." He scratched the back of his neck. "Was there anything else in the room?"

"This bottle. Watch it. When I looked at it with the mage sight, it about burned my eyes out." Larry picked the proffered bottle out of my hand and examined it closely, "Doesn't seem to be magick at all. Are you sure this is what you're talking about?"

I reluctantly opened my other eye and looked again. There was nothing bright or powerful about the bottle at all. It was just a stoppered metallic glass bottle. What the hell? "Wait," I said. "The time I looked at it I think it didn't have a stopper."

Larry pulled the stopper, and I went blind from the bright nimbus that sprang forth. Larry swore and dropped the bottle. He shook his head to clear it, then picked the bottle back up, hastily putting the stopper back in place. "That was a nasty surprise! I'm still blinking spots from my vision." Larry held the bottle with one hand and rubbed his eyes with the other.

Mischief had bolted the moment the bottle was unstopped and I found him under my desk. *I no go there, it very bad, bad predator!* He shivered so hard I thought he would faint.

Bad? How is it bad, Mischief? I mentally asked the *Imrit*. He just shivered and refused to move or answer, staring back towards the room, whimpering in abject terror. Mischief wrapped around my leg in an eye-blink as I stood up, knocking me off-balance. Luckily, I managed to grab the desk before I fell over.

No go back herd sister! No! I hold you here! Mischief dug in her paws, and anchored herself in some way. It was like trying to pull my foot out of a bear trap. I couldn't pull free from her. "Mischief! Let go!" I was practically screaming at the *Imrit*.

Zhirk looked in on us to see what the commotion was and saw me trying to pull away from the terrified *Imrit*, he started chuckling, and earned himself a hard glare from me. He raised his hands and went back into the outer office with Larry, and soon I heard chuckles from both of them.

"Let! Go!" I finally shouted and the *Imrit* meekly, slowly, and very reluctantly released me. *I'll be fine*, I told Mischief, and went back to the outer office.

The *Imrit* wailed incoherently, but would not leave the place under the desk, so terrified he was. Larry had recovered his sight, and Zhirk stood off to one side as he watched the goings on, out of the way and ready should Baldy make an entrance. We hadn't forgotten about him, and I'm sure he was thinking about us.

"OK, let's try that again." Larry uncorked the bottle. A wail of pure terror came from the inner office from Mischief, and I quickly closed the door.

"Can you tell what has got Mischief so terrified, Larry?" I asked as he murmured a spell to protect his eyes and opened his sight once more. "The bottle had a sort of suction to it. It was hanging off the man who tried to use it on me, and it was like he went away. There just was no one home."

"Really, no one home, eh? Well, little thief, let's have a better look at you, shall we?" Larry mumbled at the bottle as he placed it on the floor outside the casting circle.

"Can you show me that trick with the eyes? I'd like to watch what you're doing."

"Certainly," he said absentmindedly, and then gave me a quick description of the method.

I started to put the mental pieces together when Larry gasped and looked at me in panic. "Shield me!" he choked out. I quickly thought of a wall and tried to bring it forth. This was personal magick so I could do it, but it taxed me hard. I imagined the wall. Its impenetrability. Its solidity. Mentally, brick by brick I built it around Larry. The mental image rose past his eyes, when he suddenly relaxed. As he dropped his spell, I dropped mine, and felt the remnants drawn away into the bottle. I shivered and took an involuntary step back from it. Larry was pale, and shaking. I'd never seen him even close to uncomfortable, and here he was with a full on panic.

"Oh my god! That was horrible!" he said like the frightened man that he was. "It was eating me! Oh my god! It did eat part of me! What the hell is that thing!" Mischief wailed again from under the desk, a fearful counterpoint to Larry's own cries. "Larry!" I shook him to get his attention. He didn't even react. I hauled back and slapped him across the face. That woke him from his shock. He looked at me with haunted eyes.

"That thing," he said, "started to eat my soul. I sent a touch of magick to it and it started sucking my magick and my soul out of me, like a kid sucking a strand of spaghetti. I couldn't stop it once it started, it was so horrid. I've lost a part of myself and I can't get it back!"

He collapsed and hugged his arms across his body and started rocking back and forth. Out of curiosity, I used my other sight to look at him. He was noticeably dimmer, and I could see what looked like a gaping tear in his aura — no wonder he hurt so! Most of him was still there, but a large portion, like a big bite from a hamburger, was missing. I shuddered. To live that way for the rest of your life, knowing that what you are would never be what you were.

I turned to Larry, and lifted his chin with my hand. "Larry, focus! We need to know what that thing is. Can you do it?" He looked at me, still dazed.

"That thing eats souls, Fern. It will eat your whole soul if you let it. Why I don't know and I'm not staying in the room with it. That thing is evil! The only reason anyone would want something like that would be to kill someone. Destroy it! If you can't do that, lose it somewhere deep. Fill it with iron filings and throw it in some deep place so no one will find it."

I pushed him since I needed to know about the circle. "Larry, what about the circle, how does it fit? Is it part of the circle?" He looked at me like I was crazed or fanatical, and maybe I was at that moment. But I did know that the way people handle a shock is to get moving on something else. That way you can hold off things until you're ready to deal.

He focused back on the little bottle, and stared at it like one would looking down the end of a loaded gun. "It sucks people's lives into it, all of them. I can't feel myself any more so I...... I think it converts the soul," he said, and hugged himself harder. "I think it converts the soul to energy. Maybe to be used by the owner. But I don't know how you'd make the bottle release the energy." He focused harder as he thought about the problem. I saw him relax a fraction as he studied the circle.

"Each of those represent the bottle maybe, which means the fifth ingredient would have to also."

He looked at me again, and over at Zhirk. "This is the circle as you saw it, eh?", he said, his voice starting to tremble again. "Everything seems to me to say the bottle is either in the circle or on the point of the circle. I'd guess in the circle, which still gives us a mystery as to what the fifth one still is. Are the ingredients in the correct arrangement on the circle?"

"Yes", I said at the same time Zhirk said "No". He looked at me and Larry. "The mandrake and the mushroom are switched. The flower and the mushroom were on the points farthest away from the open point, and the Mandrake and the Bladderwort on the two closest to the open one." He tapped his head. "Oral tradition for trolls remember? Memory practice. We have to or no history gets saved."

We rearranged the circle, Larry looked again. "Put the bottle in the center. Uh, the cork's in it, right?" I hastily picked up the cork, then jammed it home in the bottle's mouth.

"Okay, Zhirk could you stand on that last point for me?" he said to the big troll.

Zhirk stepped warily to the point. Larry leaned over to me and said, "See anything? Look real close at the position of everything." I did as he asked and looked at the whole thing with the other sight but didn't see what he was talking about, and said so to him.

"The circle is a conduit," he said. "I think a person stands like Zhirk at the open point and is the fifth ingredient. She or he casts the spell and the bottle somehow transfers the stored power to the caster."

"It can also be used to power spells or drain the essence from true entities if you know how," came a deep voice that crackled like parchment. Mischief wailed in terror as an aura of menace washed over us. Baldy was there in the doorway to the inner office.

16

Z HIRK SPUN AND CHARGED IN ONE MOTION. Baldy just reached over with fluid, inhuman speed and snatched one of Zhirk's shotguns off the floor. He casually aimed one-handed from the hip, and blew the left half of his face away. Mischief tore through my coat pocket in blind terror and vanished under the bookcase.

Zhirk jerked upright, and trembled, the body shaking as nerves overloaded and fired at random with no brain to coordinate them. Then he toppled onto his side, and fell like a cut tree. Blood splashed all over the wall as his heart refused to get the message, and continued to pump blood from his ruined face, soaking the futon.

I started to take a step and Baldy's parchment-like voice cracked like a whip. "Don't move! Don't you even move! You," he growled at Larry, "on your belly now, no sudden moves." He looked at me, and said with quiet viciousness, "You, girl, take these." He threw some plastic zip strips next to the prone Larry. "Do his wrists and ankles. Then a third one to tie the first two together. Quick now, or I make your young man look like the troll." I glanced over at Zhirk, who was still twitching, and pumping blood in weakening spurts onto the blood-soaked futon.

Once I had done as he asked, he ordered me to the ground and trussed me up like he had me do to Larry. I looked at Larry, who was wide-eyed with shock. He was in no shape for anything. I looked at Baldy, who was fastidiously polishing the stoppered bottle. "I was very annoyed with the two of you for invading my abode," Baldy said matter-of-factly. He took a step to move in front of me, then squatted onto his heels and stared me in the eyes.

"But then you build my circle here for me to use, and give me such a wonderful place to reside. I'm going to enjoy my stay here. Thank you for loaning me your place." He smiled but, as the cliché goes, it never reached his eyes. His eyes were hungry, and we were steak set in front of a starving man.

He plucked the stopper from the bottle, then straightened and stepped over to where Larry lay. "Do you know how this little thing works? Of course you do," he said condescendingly. "I was listening and gaped in absolute amazement at your man's tremendous deductive powers," Larry's eyes locked on the bottle as Baldy rolled it between his fingers like a magician. Fear rolled off him like a wave, and Mischief wailed in utter terror from somewhere nearby.

He smirked at Larry, then turned towards Zhirk's body, "Oh you had a little help from your friend here," and he slid his toes under the body, then flipped over. Zhirk's earthly remains landed with a wet, heavy thud on its back. "But oh so sad, he's dead now, and no help is he?" He giggled like a child and that scared me even more than the ranting. Baldy was completely deranged.

He dipped his fingers in Zhirk's blood. He waved them under his nose, shivering in pleasure. Baldy stepped to the circle, and began slowly re-tracing it. Where the blood touched the chalked outline, it began to glow and smoke. He mumbled continuously through the casting and, when he was done, the circle was re-written in blood burned into the wood floor. Baldy added a circle of symbols outside the pattern.

He then looked at Larry and me. "Oh the things I am going to share with the two of you," he said, and it sounded like a cat's purr. The kind when it has a helpless animal it is playing with. He dabbed blood on the back of my neck and on each ear and eyelid, mumbling in some language I couldn't understand. I wanted to scream from the ice-cold touch of his fingers. My body settled for dry heaves. He chuckled, and moved over to Larry, who looked like he was catatonic. His eyes were wide and blank. He was breathing faster than I'd ever heard before. Baldy repeated the process as Larry whimpered. There was the smell of urine and feces. Baldy laughed out loud, then dabbed himself the same way.

"I've not been so annoyed by you ephemeral creatures in a long time, and I want to really show you how much I appreciate being able to extract a little revenge," he said to us, then bent and checked the zip-ties, adding a second set to the first. "Don't go anywhere, I have something I want to show you when I get back, and I want a captive audience." Baldy opened the front door and stepped through. The door closed behind him, leaving Larry and me in the room with the smoking, bloody casting circle.

Larry started dry-heaving, and thrashed against the bonds, but couldn't escape them. After a short time, he stopped struggling and lay still. I tried to get loose, but couldn't and the more apparent it became that I wasn't going to escape, the more frantic I became. I didn't want to die here. I didn't want to die at all. And it looked increasingly like that is exactly what was going to happen to Larry and me when Baldy got back. I started thinking about what he said when he left.

Larry suddenly screamed. The wail of horror went for as long as he had breath, then silence and he'd gather a lungful of air, and scream again. It went on until he was hoarse. After he went hoarse, his shoulders started to shake, and I heard weeping sounds. That actually perked me up a little, crying meant he was probably lucid enough to talk to.

"Larry, can you hear me?" The sobbing kept going for a moment, then a faint 'uh huh'. He sounded like a lost child. I bit back a sympathetic reply. I needed him lucid, not a dependent kid.

"What do you think he left for?"

"I dunno."

"Larry, why did he leave?"

His response was a little surly this time. "I Dunno."

"Larry you beanpole asshat! What do you think he's doing?!"

He hunched over, then spit the words out bitterly. "What the hell do you think it means, Fernie! He's going to get someone to kill in front of us!" He stopped and took a breath. "Are you really that stupid that you couldn't figure it out on your own, you got to ask me for all the damn details all the damn time?"

I wanted to hit him, but that's always what I want to do when I'm scared. Having him mad made me feel like I wasn't alone. I focused, and slowly reached mentally for Mischief. *Can you hear me herd friend? I need your help. Please herd friend, come help me.* I felt it under the bookcase, and felt its paralyzing terror at the magick and the smell of Zhirk's blood.

I can't, it wailed mentally, *I can't I afraid, I can't! I can't! I can't!*

I exploded at it like Larry did at me. *You little worthless miserable…!* I caught myself, and then put all the mental strength into a command, *Come here!*

Mischief moved jerkily out from under the bookcase, and literally fought me the whole way. The bond allowed me to command it, but this would ruin any trust we built up. I'd never get an *Imrit* to work with me again, but screw that, I wanted to live! Mischief wailed in absolute terror as I forced him to come to me.

The blood drove her into a frenzy of fear that almost slipped her from my control. But his desperation wasn't strong enough, and I finally pulled *Imrit* to my side. '*Chew the plastic, free me.*' It bit the plastic strips in a frenzy, and soon I was able to break the restraint and free myself.

I went to my desk in the inner office and retrieved a pocket knife and cut Larry free. The *Imrit* still quivered in fear at where I was last bound. I picked Mischief up, and we left the office and sprinted to my car. A short panicked drive later, we were back at Larry's store. He immediately ran to the back and began a protective casting about himself in his back room.

Mischief chose at that time to come out of his stupor and began wildly fighting me. I dropped him and the *Imrit* scrambled to a darker section of the store and hid. *You predator! You lie! You no friend! You predator! I hate you!* Its rage and fear made my heart speed up as the echo of the bond still tugged faintly as it faded. *I am sorry, herd-sister. I needed you. Now you are free.* I severed the bond mentally and let it return to its own world. There were bigger problems than a pissed-off *Imrit*.

Larry tried to power up his hastily drawn circle and collapsed gagging and retching. "Larry! What's happening?" I said rather inanely. The adrenalin was wearing off and I was feeling pretty spacey, so I wasn't really focusing well.

Then the points that Baldy placed on me flared to life, and I felt his exultation, heard the sounds of the screaming child he had trapped. There was a sudden, disorienting shift, and I was seeing through his eyes the girl as he placed the bottle's mouth against her forehead and drained away her life, and her soul. The child's eyes went glassy, and Baldy dropped her like a forgotten toy. The parents were screaming as he grabbed the next child, who squalled in fear. I tried to shut out the images as he did the same to the rest of the family he'd captured, draining each one with the bottle.

I joined Larry on the floor retching, the images oozing like rotted slime across my brain. The only word I could put to the horror and disgust is rape. Baldy had raped my mind, and my soul. I could feel him, and his glee at creating such misery and despair. I thought he could probably feel us as well. We had to get rid of the marks.

Larry thought the same thing apparently. He drunkenly pushed himself off the floor, and stumbled over to the Christian section of his store. He knocked books, crystals, and candles to the floor in clumsy haste. Then he whimpered and grabbed a green bottle off the shelf. He pulled the cork, and then drew his handkerchief from his back pocket. The liquid spilled from the bottle soaking the cloth, and he rubbed frantically at his eyes. I felt a slight 'click' and Larry poured the water on his neck as he rubbed his ears. There were two more 'clicks' and I felt a hot flash of rage spear me between the eyes, and I collapsed on the floor.

The images flashed with bright neon intensity through me. I tried shutting my eyes and covering my ears in a vain attempt to keep the sights and sounds out. Baldy kept slashing at me mentally, trying to force my eyes open. Thankfully, that suddenly stopped as water was poured on my head. I felt two sharp pains on my eyelids, and one on the back of my neck. Larry pried my hands away from my ears and rubbed quickly with the wet handkerchief. There was a flare of pain and a 'clicking' sensation, as the link Baldy had forged to me broke.

I shook my head to clear the last of the viscous sludge from my thoughts and looked at Larry. "What was that stuff anyway?"

"Holy water. I've got gallons of the stuff in the back. I get a priest from the local Episcopal Church to come by every weekend and bless the water drum I have set up. If I'm going to sell holy water in the store, I've got to have truth in advertising." He wiped his forehead and looked at me.

"I never want to feel that again. That…" He shivered, then looked at me. I could feel his anger and outrage spring up like a wildfire. His whole demeanor changed. He'd had enough. It was a shock to see it happen, I think I just watched him for a full minute. Larry returned the gaze, then a faint smile actually formed on his haunted features.

"So what's next, then?" I started to reply as my heart lurched. No! I couldn't break down now. We weren't safe. I fought my own desire to just let go and mourn. Zhirk was gone. The shock was wearing off.

This shop was Larry's, and he felt more in control here. That helps a lot when you're messed up like we were. Offices like mine, and shops like Larry's, don't really have a threshold, because all the people coming and going mixes everything up. That's why homes and thresholds have such meaning in folklore. Home is a strong place of personal magick, and a threshold is the barrier that protects the home. The longer you live in a place, the harder it is for anything to bring magick into your home. Mortal wizards can come in, if they're invited. No wizard can forcibly enter another's home without an invitation.

We were very vulnerable here. We needed a place to hide, and time to figure our next move. Larry's relief had knocked the numbness away. He was trying to purge the horror, and on an instinctual level, I was too. We couldn't. Not here. Not now. I bit my lip so hard it bled. The pain helped me drive the grief back into the little box, at least for now.

"We go somewhere else," I told him quickly. "Your house ought to be safe enough for the moment. We can plan what to do there. I'll call Fawn and warn her about Baldy." I grabbed Larry by the arm and dragged him out to the car before he had any chance to protest. We had to stay moving. I was too easy to trace. Baldy had a whole roomful of personal items that he could use to track me. There had to be some way to divert the locating spells that would be used.

"You know any quick obscuring spells? The ones I know require a circle and an hour's prep to work. We need to hide. Now."

"Give me some time, I'll see," he said absently. He was starting to zone out again, trying to mentally shut down from all the horror.

I grabbed him by the elbow and turned him to me. I didn't like the idea, but Larry was male, and it was time to use some female persuasion to get help. Otherwise we'd both die. I placed my hand gently on his other elbow and stepped in closer. I looked straight into his eyes and pushed myself close against him.

"Larry," I said as gently as possible, "I need you to help me, I can't figure this out fast enough alone. You have experience with this that I can only dream of. Can you help me, please?"

I about gagged on the lines as I said them. I hate manipulating friends like that. Thankfully, I could feel Larry focus, and pull himself back into the real world again. Say what you will, but guys really focus when they've got a girl to save.

It's part of their nature, or at least it's part of the good one's nature, even though nowadays it's offputting to most of us.

Larry showed me the way back to his place and we hurriedly set up a circle. He built an obscuring spell using the circle as an anchor, much like I'd done with Anne and Megan. He went to the front door and poured some Holy Water on the threshold and did the same to each window and in the house. He returned and sat in the circle.

"That should cover our butts for a while, and with me at home, the magickal wards and the Holy Water should hurt him if he tries to come in," Larry said.

"What else should we be doing?" I asked him.

"I like killing him, personally. That would just feel good right now." Larry hunched up as he said it, and tried to shrug. It looked more like a flinch than a shrug. "Other than that, break that bottle. He can't use it if it's broke."

"Broke is good," I agreed with him. "That might be better than killing him. So how do we do it? The bottle I mean?"

"I'm not sure. It would depend on the bottle itself, what it is made of, and if there's any magick holding it together," he said. "With the kind of major magick it probably has, it may be pretty fragile, even if it's been strengthened magickally. That major kind of magick always seems to be hard on things. I think it's the Order/Chaos argument myself."

I put both hands on the sides of his head and kissed him soundly. He stiffened in surprise, then I felt him relax. His arms came up and encircled me. I felt myself relax against him as our kiss deepened. It went on as we clung to each other, both of us needing the intimacy as a defense against all the horror Baldy had thrown upon us. The little box in my heart tried to open, and I ruthlessly stomped it. There was no time to mourn. There was just the kiss.

I had to come up for air first. That would guarantee his focus. Now he had a real reason for his thoughts, both magickal and, well, otherwise. I told you, I'm not a nice girl. This is how you get a guy to focus, and we needed focus. Everything I said to Larry about what he knew and what I didn't was unvarnished truth, with a hint of sex behind it. We needed ideas and plans to survive.

Larry turned on his computer, then went hunting the websites to find any references to the bottle or spells that would be placed on a bottle to make it suck souls. After about three hours of pseudo-science and dead-ends, Larry stood up, rubbed the back of his neck angrily, then slapped his hand against the desk in frustration.

"Dammit." Larry growled at the computer. "If we only knew something about him or that damn bottle, maybe we could get an edge."

"Oh, damn, I think I got an answer!" I said excitedly. "Uncle Todd told me that the demon they called up was named Semjaza."

"Semjaza?! Your parents called up a fucking DEMON!?" Larry shrieked at me. "What were your parents, errrn, never mind that." He ducked his head. "Sorry." He looked up when I didn't answer immediately.

"Yeah, 's okay. I'm... it's okay." I wanted to scream, and settled for clenching my jaw until it hurt. I nodded, then he returned it. He turned to face the computer. "You sure of that name?" he said quietly.

My folks. It was tough to think of them. I tried to recall their faces and came up blank. That bothered me maybe more than it should have. It could have been the stress of the last half-hour. I was still jittery from the adrenalin dump. "Yeah, I just didn't think about it until you said that. Uncle Todd said Semjaza. That's unusual enough to remember."

"Let's look up Semjaza and see if there's something that we can use." Larry stepped over to his computer, "Internet makes things so easy to find stuff." He chuckled grimly. I felt a wash of relief. He was starting to sound more like the old Larry. "You know how it's spelled?" he said as we waited for the machine to power up.

Once the computer was operating, we soon had a couple of links open and were reading up on Semjaza. We got a load of information from the online encyclopedias. Semjaza was the name for the leader of the *Grigorii,* or 'watchers' that were assigned by God to watch over mankind. Those *Grigorii* that lusted after human women and mated with them became 'Fallen Angels'. The offspring from these unions were called *Nephilim,* or 'Fallen Ones'. They were also called *Anakim.*

These beings were gifted with varied powers, and some were gigantic in size, towering to twelve meters in height. Because they were different, and invariably killed the woman birthing them, they were driven out of their communities, or exposed as babes in the hopes they would die. This treatment caused many of them to hate humanity. Those took great delight in creating misery wherever they went. Others compounded the horror by feasting on human flesh. Many battles were fought on the earth before the power of the *Nephilim* and *Anakim* were finally broken. The renegade immortals were banished from the face of the world.

After the Angels and sons of Adam locked the *Nephilim* and *Anakim* in the earth, God caused the flood of Noah and wiped out any landmarks to show where the *Nephilim* and their offspring were buried. This all was listed in the *Book of Enoch.* The information went on to say that *Semjaza,* or *Semyaza,* had a son *Ahiah,* who was foremost among the *Anakim,* and would be the one called forth to pave the way after *Semjaza* marked 'two children of Eve' and invested their lives with power.

Ahiah would be drawn forth to the power and then sacrifice the two women to break the seal on *Semjaza's* prison. He would then travel the earth, and release other *Nephilim*. *Ahiah's* power would come from a vessel carried by *Ahiah* that could use the essence of any of the *Nephilim's* descendants to fill it for the ritual.

"*Ahiah* has to be the opener, and the gateway for *Semjaza* if this stuff is accurate," Larry said as he studied the links.

"With the bottle being the battery to power everything?" I asked.

He tapped the keys, setting the file displays side-by-side. "It feels as if none of the links is actually a reference and they're just cycling through each other. Let's look through some more of them to be sure that they just aren't circle jerking ourselves off here."

We went through twelve more links and read up on *Semjaza*, *Ahiah*, and the *Book of Enoch*. Finally, we came away convinced that what we had was probably accurate. We were staking our lives on 'likely' and 'probable'. They could carve that on our headstones if we were wrong.

I stayed at the house, while Larry went by his store. I was afraid to get out of the circle, and let that thing figure out where we were. More, I was trying very hard not to let all that horror with Zhirk out of the box. It is so, so hard to keep grief locked away.

I felt ill when Larry finally returned after about a half-hour. He'd gotten more holy water from the store and had picked up a few silver crucifixes for the both of us, plus a few other items he thought might be handy. All that time he was exposed. If that thing could track him, we'd been made. I had to think ambush, we were heading into an ambush. Hey, it's not paranoia if they are out to get you, it's survival instinct.

All the way over to my office, the information swirled in my head. Was Baldy actually *Ahiah* that the legend talked about? It made a weird sort of sense, but how did *Ahiah* tie into Hervald? Why the attacks on the girls? Was Hervald chosen or did he just find that bottle? Lots of questions and not very many answers yet. We got to my office in time to see Baldy head up the steps. Larry slowed the car. I could feel him tense up as he spotted Baldy.

My heart was in my throat as I watched him. Zhirk's limp body was suddenly in my mind. I bit my lip to keep from screaming, scrunching my eyes closed and forcing my panic back in the box. All the while praying we weren't seen.

Baldy ignored us, or maybe didn't see us, and disappeared inside the building. Larry pulled into the parking lot and then turned to me.

"Fernie, do we really want to be here?" When I didn't answer, he started sounding a little panicky. "Are you really thinking of going in guns blazing? You saw what he did to Zhirk." He took a shaky breath. "I vote we make tracks for Australia."

"I got one for you, how about we call Fawn and the TAC team, and we all go pay Baldy a visit?" I felt my mouth curl into a particularly nasty smile.

Larry looked at me like I'd gone off the rails. He stared at me, then looked back at the building. He squared his shoulders, then it was like listening to a televangelist giving a sermon. "I am a new convert to the true belief of excessive firepower. Especially after what we've gone through."

It sounded like Larry had had enough of being a target. I was way past my quota. I called Fawn and informed her where Baldy was, and what he was likely trying to do. I didn't tell her about the *Nephilim* stuff. That would be when we were face-to-face, and could talk without being overheard. Some instinct in me didn't want people to know about that.

We waited in Larry's car until TAC van arrived. Fawn had pulled out all the stops. Patrol cars stopped in the streets, surrounding and isolating the building. With all the firepower we saw, it was certain the officers were keeping a tight perimeter. Fawn saw us and waved us through the perimeter. She was in full TAC gear: armored vest, FN-FAL, and a silver sword for backup. As we reached the back of the van, she looked up, a grim smile on her features. She WANTED this guy. I almost felt sorry for Baldy. Almost.

"So, Shorty, have you moved anything around since I was in there the last time?" she questioned, as the TAC team checked their gear.

"Yeah, I moved a few pieces. If you've got a piece of paper or something to draw on, I can give you the layout."

Fawn unbuttoned a pouch, then pulled out a notebook and a pen. She handed it to me. I drew the inside of the room as it was with Zhirk's bedroll against a wall and the circle on the floor in the outer office. I think my hand shook as I finished, and gave Fawn back her notebook. She glanced at it for a moment.

"Huh, looks pretty much the same. Thanks." She called the team over. They double-timed it to her and huddled over the drawing. She gave each one instructions, tapping the map to indicate the position. Once they'd gone over it twice, she stood up and told the team leaders to look it over again for anything that had been missed on the first go-round.

Fawn left the group, and walked back to Larry and I. "Okay you two, stay here until we go through it. Fernie, I'm going to have my cell phone on so you can follow us through, tell us if anything's off or been moved," she said crisply to me as she put her ear camera-phone on.

She spoke my number into the phone, and it was 'TAC live with Fawn'. Fawn was to be the observer and leader of the backup team for the TAC unit. We settled down by the TAC van, and watched on the big monitor in the back. The lead unit worked its way upstairs, and Fawn coordinated the placement of the backup unit. Once in place, with the reserve unit at the stairwell door, the first team blew my door of its hinges and charged into the room.

Baldy was there. Zhirk's body and the circle were there too. I saw Baldy on the first team's lead camera. One moment, he was frozen in shock, looking for all the world like that actor, Max Shreck, from 'Nosferatu'. Then he laughed, and turned to the TAC team. He walked towards them, as if he hadn't a care in the world. The TAC team opened up. I could hear the staccato gunfire over the cellphone. Baldy continued to laugh as he stepped through the hail of bullets like it didn't exist.

The bullets never seemed to touch him as he reached the TAC team leader. The guy was no coward, but was not the quickest thinker. After seeing Baldy walk though gunfire to right in front of him, the guy tried to knock him down with a kick. Baldy just grabbed his harness, then placed the bottle on the officer's cheek. We watched him just go limp like a rag doll. Baldy crooned words I didn't understand and reached for a second man as the team leader fell limply to the ground.

The others didn't play hero, but ran for the stairs as if the devil herself was right behind them. Baldy had caught the last man out the door at the top of the steps and placed the bottle against his neck. The officer dropped a flash bang he'd pulled off his belt to cover the retreat. It fell at Baldy's feet and detonated. He yowled in surprise and pain from the bright light, and disappeared back into the depths of my office.

So we had a temporary standoff. Us on the outside, Baldy in my office. While Fawn was coordinating the teams, Baldy ended the temporary part. He kicked the plywood off the broken window. Baldy leapt from the window, arced over the street, landed on the adjoining building, and disappeared in a burst of speed.

I charged up the stairs. Fawn and Larry followed, and the three of us moved to my office while the TAC team and the regular officers tried to locate and contain Baldy. Fawn took me over by my desk, which resembled Swiss cheese after the gunfight. Zhirk's body had been torn up by the panicked gunfire. I turned my back to it to keep from throwing up, and forced my grief into a small black hole in my heart.

Fawn motioned Larry over, then took a deep breath that got Larry's attention. She exhaled shakily. "I've never seen anything like that, ever. What are we playing with here, Shorty?"

I hesitated as Fawn looked at me. Larry looked anywhere except at the two of us. We were in a very dangerous situation. We didn't have a real clue as to motive beyond what we found on the 'net, and somehow Fawn and especially me, were caught up in the middle of this and part and parcel of the whole thing.

"We really need to talk in private, Fawn. Please. The sooner the better," Larry said quietly. Fawn looked at Larry. I could see her wrestling with the desire to get Baldy, and, something else.

She finally sighed. "Okay, where?"

Larry shrugged uneasily. "How about we get someplace safer than here? I think my place is compromised. I don't want to trust that he doesn't know about it. With him busy eluding the police, we can find a place to hide and get behind a casting circle and he won't be able to find us."

Fawn nodded. "I'll join you after we put the team back in the barn."

17

S INCE LARRY FELT HIS PLACE WAS NO LONGER SAFE, Fawn piled us in the back of her car and took us to her small house on the outskirts of Dartmouth. Larry got busy once inside, and traced an irregular casting circle in the kitchen around the tables and to the entry in the pantry. As he worked, Fawn dragged a chair out from the two-person kitchen table and gestured to the other one. "How about talking about everything since the start of this whole mess, short stuff. A recap if you like. I'm kind of an involved outsider to all that's been happening."

My heart lurched as Zhirk came into my mind. I gritted my teeth and forced the feeling back. It was not time to let go, not yet. I gathered my thoughts, then launched into the story. I took a few deep breaths, then recounted my experiences starting with Hervald, going to Rynun, and meeting Baldy for the first time. I wanted to cry, but I wouldn't. I finished up with Uncle

Todd's story about the aborted casting and Zhirk's dying at Baldy *nee' Ahiah's* hands. Yeah, I was in part convinced that they were one and the same person.

When Larry finished with his circle, Fawn recapped her experiences with the disappearing Hervald, bottle, and Baldy. She was pretty upset about it, and more so now with Baldy killing fellow officers that she knew personally. Fawn was looking for some payback and I didn't blame her. I wanted some for Zhirk. My heart lurched again. It burned hot, so hot. I hated. I hated Baldy so much my stomach emptied itself on the floor. Larry ran to the bathroom and got a wet towel for me, and Fawn got a mop from the kitchen.

After cleaning up the mess, Larry asked if anyone knew more about the ritual we were in. "You make it sound like the ritual was still operating until they, umm, stopped it. But from what you both have said, it sounds more like it's still operating, at least to me. If that's the case, maybe all this would stop if you could really complete the spell or banish it," he said musingly. He looked at the two of us. "At least it will change something,

"Yeah, but how?" I said back acidly. "We could be really shooting ourselves in the foot if we're not careful." He moved over to place his hands on the back of Fawn's chair. "Well, why don't we ask your Uncle Todd a few more questions about the spell? If you want straight answers, you go ask the right questions of the right people."

Fawn nodded as Larry finished. "Good idea, maybe we missed something." She looked at the circle Larry had drawn on her floor and carpet, and her face fell. "I really don't want to clean that up. If we live through this, Larry Potter, you're cleaning up this mess." I didn't want to leave the circle, but we needed more information. Reluctantly, we left Fawn's house and drove to Uncle Todd's.

Uncle Todd came out on the lawn as we pulled up. He threw his arms wide to hug us and Fawn and I grabbed him, hustling him back into the house. Larry immediately started making a new circle while Fawn and I moved Uncle Todd to his recliner. We both sat down on the small sofa as Larry feverishly drew the protection circle.

"Uncle Todd," Fawn started, "Is there anything beyond the story that you might have forgotten to add in? That guy is definitely after Fern, and maybe me." Larry finished the circle and mumbled a quick spell to activate it. Uncle Todd looked at both of us, then shook his head slowly as Larry joined us on the sofa. It'd have even been fun if we weren't so wrapped up in, you know, trying not to be killed. "I don't know all the details of the spell, Fern. Your folks didn't write all of it down," he said slowly.

I was ready to take him at his word, but Larry jumped right on Uncle Todd verbally. "You're lying and you're scared that we're going to find out what it is," Larry snapped angrily at him. "You know exactly what they were trying to do, and it scared you spitless. Now I can pull it out of you or you can tell us what it is. Either way we will know and, more importantly, we HAVE to know. That thing out there is after both of them. They'll die and their souls will be destroyed if that thing gets the bottle on them."

He took in just enough breath for another verbal charge. "So make up your mind quickly. Mine is, and you'll tell us what's really going on, one peaceful way, or a very painful other." Larry stood up, power emanating from him. I could feel my forearms and neck goose pimple from the sensation.

It wasn't as much as Larry had before the bottle sucked him, to be sure, but Larry KNEW how to use what he had. He had spent the time to learn the ins and outs of magick as was currently known. He stared at our Uncle Todd. Both Fawn and I moved off the couch away from the two men. I wanted to tell Larry to lay off. But if what he accused Uncle Todd of was true, then we needed him to come clean and tell us the real story. "We're waiting, Mr. Fatelli. Which is it going to be?"

Uncle Todd looked like he wanted to shrink into himself and disappear. His eyes were so big and unfocused, it looked like he had fled his body. He started to hunch over and tears spilled from his eyes, and he began to rock back and forth. Larry took one quick step and slapped him hard across the face. I automatically took a stride and punched Larry in the kidney, putting him down.

"Don't you do that to him!" I screamed at him. "Don't you touch him like that!"

I was grabbed and tossed on the couch by Fawn. I jumped off ready to go after Larry again. She pushed me back onto it as Larry got up and looked at my now very angry uncle.

"Shorty, Larry's right. Todd is hiding something, and we need to know what," she told me. When I didn't answer, she grabbed me with both her hands and pulled me into a tight hug. She spoke softly in my ear, as I was held, feet a full six inches off the ground, in her bear hug. "Sis, we need to know. Todd's the only one who remembers that night at all. I don't. You don't. Larry wasn't there. Uncle Todd's the only eyewitness. He's the only one who knows the truth."

I fought a little more, but it was token resistance for the ego. Fawn and Larry were right, dammit. It hurt to think that Uncle Todd had lied to me. But family can hurt you the most with the least effort. That's always been true. I sat back down after Fawn released me, and glared daggers at all three of them. Uncle Todd looked at me, and dropped his eyes guiltily. "I'm sorry girls," he began. "I'm so sorry. I just couldn't face it. He shook his head as tears streamed down his cheek. "I'd hoped I never would have to talk about this." Larry took a step at Uncle Todd, glowering as if he was ready to launch himself at him.

"Quit delaying then and get to the bloody explanation, eh? It's bad enough already without being a drama-boy." Larry said callously. "Get on with it or I'll rip it out of you."

I started to get up, and then sat down again as Fawn gave me a warning glare. Larry was a whiz at reading people, I needed to remember that. He saw something that I didn't, and he's leaning on Uncle Todd because it's the only way to get the truth and we need the truth, all of it, the ugly parts too. Perhaps especially the ugly parts. Uncle Todd drew a shuddering breath. His voice was empty, almost hollow as he spoke.

"I have to go back to the start of the casting. That's where we went wrong. It was the entire casting really. Your mother wanted to be sure to never have you get sick again, and your father wanted you protected from anything that might come calling after such a casting was done."

He looked at us. "The thing was that in order for the casting to work, and because of who they were going to steal power from, you two girls had to die at the moment of the casting, and I, I was supposed to kill you two. I was supposed to do it by taping a bag over your heads and smothering you."

He paused here as he hugged himself. I was sickened. Mom and Dad wanting to kill us? So they could save us? That was just too perverse to get my head around. All I could do was listen as Uncle Todd launched back into his story.

"One thing about magick like your folks were using. It needed potential. If you died from the disease, the potential of your life would be dissipated naturally with the disease, nothing to pull power from or to. But if you died suddenly in an accident, or by someone's intent, then power was there to be used in the spells.

"It could be called also as an anchor, at least that's what your father told me." Uncle Todd swallowed and continued. "I think they had gotten so far into the research that they didn't realize how horrific this was. They got swallowed by the evil in it and didn't even think about what they were doing. Your mom wanted you so badly to live. She was willing to do anything to keep you."

Todd looked at Fawn, who looked back at him like when you find a dangerous snake underfoot. She, like me, was horrified by the story. Todd continued, his voice cracking with emotion. "I was scared to do what they asked but scared of what might happen to me if I didn't. So I put the bags over your heads but didn't tape them tightly. I kept two fingers between your throats and the plastic, and prayed it was enough to keep you from smothering."

He paused, eyes haunted. Tears glistened, and he used his sleeve to wipe them away. "When the spell was started, you two had to be dead. I thought about trying to sneak you both to the car, but your mother saw me. She had me put you both on the pentacle. When you were hit with the spell and the power started into you, *Semjaza* went berserk, and tried to claim all of us. I didn't think. The power coming from that thing was so evil. I just grabbed you two and ran for the car. I tore the bags off and tossed you both in the back seat."

"I could have saved them, but after getting you girls in the car, I couldn't go back for them. They were screaming. That thing was screaming and cursing. I drove and didn't stop." He paused, and took a breath as he glanced at Larry who motioned him to hurry it up. "Ruthie and I did wall the power away from you, but that spell was never finished." He shrugged. "It didn't get banished, I think. I can still feel it in the auras your aunt and I bound to you to protect you. Those wards would have dissipated if the spell had broken down."

I looked at Fawn. She had stood next to Larry and had intertwined her hand in his. They stood there like they belonged with each other, taking strength and giving it to each other through simple contact.

"Why are you holding hands like that?"

Both of them started, then Larry got a sheepish smile on his face. "You haven't told her yet?" He looked at Fawn.

"Told me what?!" I said, angry at the fact everyone else knew something I didn't. They both just smiled at me in such a way that it grated on my nerves. Both of them, the same smile. Then it hit me like a blinding light! I think my mouth flapped like a fish's out of water. "Y-you're, dating?!" Everything fell in place. That was what Fawn had been trying to tell me those days ago. And I had been playing Larry, correction, *thought* I had been playing Larry like a fish on a hook.

"We're getting married," my sister said, confirming my guess. "I tried to tell you earlier, but you've been a crazy woman since this started, so I really didn't get a chance to." She looked over at Larry, and he looked at me after a moment, and I felt my face and ears flush hot. Dammit I hate being embarrassed!

Uncle Todd brought us back to reality. "Listen, I'm really proud for you two, but there's real life out there trying to kill you. So how about we concentrate on that, okay?" he said quietly. The happy mood soured faster than warm milk.

Todd sounded, and looked, scared. He had a right to be. If he was correct, that spell was still in suspension out there wherever he and my parents had done the casting. We were going to have to go back and either break the spell, or, finish the job by finishing the casting. Either way, I didn't like the idea of going anywhere Baldy might show up. To me, that location was all-to-likely for him to show.

We drove by Larry's shop again, and he got some silver wire, LOTS more holy water, salt, and a coil of iron wire to go with the silver. Larry also gave Fawn and me a silver cross. I put it on and tucked it under my shirt. He put the wire, water, and salt in the trunk and got ready to drive to the site.

A thought occurred to me at that point. "Uh, Uncle Todd? Who's going to take the empty space on the pentacle? I count four of us and don't we need one more?" This was going to be rough. I was certain we needed one more for the circle. Todd looked at me like I grew an extra eye in the center of my forehead, and Larry took Fawn's hand in his and sunk into thought.

"I guess we do," Larry said, conceding the point. "But who's going to volunteer for this one anyway? It's not like you can grab someone off the street and say 'we need you for a dangerous magick ritual, care to join us?' Fernie, this is going to take some thought."

"What about Rynun?" I thought quizzically.

"Who's Rynun?" asked Todd and Larry in unison. Fawn just looked at me like I was crazy.

"Err, a friend of sorts," I replied. "He's a Brown Man. Would that work for the circle?"

"If he's alive, then it should," responded Larry. "It might even help considering the stuff you supposedly got hooked into. He might actually be a good magickal 'grounding' for the spell," Larry said musingly. "Where do we find him, Fern?"

"He's nearby, just take me to Klaus's on the corner. I can do the rest easy."

18

L ARRY DROVE ME TO THE CORNER and let me out. It only took a moment to get my 'tools of persuasion'. Fawn and Larry gave me incredulous looks when I came out with three bottles of very expensive wine. They drove me back to the alleyway. I could see Rynun under his dumpster.

"Hey Rynun! Got a minute?"

"Shhhh-uuuurrre, Fuuurrrnnnyyyyyy. I guuuurrot sshhhommmmmm fuuuuur…uuuur yoooou." He crawled out from under the dumpster as I sat on my heels. I laid everything out for him before I gave him the first bottle. Hervald, Baldy/*Ahiah*, and the glass bottle.

When I wound down, he grabbed the proffered wine, and upended the bottle. He sat there, cross-legged, pouring the whole contents down his throat without swallowing. "Dammnuuuurrrp interlopers!" he belched in my face.

"Needssuuuurrp a leesonnnnnooorrrrrrph, in manners. Count me in. *hic.*" He leapt into the car, nimble as a monkey, and we were soon off and away.

Rynun was snoring lustily and the car smelled like a ripe distillery by the time we pulled into the half-hidden drive that Uncle Todd had told us about. The overgrown road had not seen much of any traffic in years. The only thing that kept us on the trail were the trees that lined it so tightly. The forest was unnaturally quiet. No birds sang, no noise permeated the woods at all. The silence was unnerving.

We drove further in, the trees bent away from our direction of travel, as if to remove themselves from whatever was at the end of the road. As we got closer to the cabin, things began to change. Trees here leaned down to almost a forty-five degree angle away from our destination. It was like a bomb blast had gone off somewhere ahead of us. The trees had bits of bark falling off, looking like wooden lepers. The few leaves that remained on limbs were a pale, sickly yellow-green.

I looked along the sides of the road as Larry drove. Here and there were a few animals on the ground between the trees. They were curled up, looking like they had just fallen asleep. "What's that?" Fawn pointed to what looked like a curled up opossum near the road. Larry slowed the car to get a better look. The opossum was dead. It's snarl of pain and fear frozen on its mummified husk.

Something had killed it and nothing would touch the body. All the animals we had seen were dead. Nothing lived here. A literal forest of the dead. Gods and outsiders, what a horrid place this was. The trees were really dead as we got to a small clearing. Just dry dead wood that littered the ground and sticks poking themselves skyward like dried fingers of a corpse's hand.

The cabin sat there in the clearing like some boxy skull of a long-dead giant. The windows, still intact, were opaque with dust. The paint on the walls had peeled away and the wood underneath gave the appearance of dried, rotted flesh peeling away from bone. I think we all shuddered to see it.

A car was sitting in front of the house on four flat tires and dust so thick upon it that it was impossible to tell the color. The malevolence of the place seemed to give the vehicle a semblance of life. The headlights, partly covered in dust and mud, seemed more to be the hooded eyes of a predator than a glass bulb. There was the feeling that the car would rear up and devour us if it could.

Rynun had stopped snoring, but was still asleep in the back as we nervously and slowly got out of the car. Wherever we stepped, a puff of dried yellowish dust rose up like some mindless blob of smoke to hover just off the ground until gravity finally reasserted itself and pulled the dust back to rest on the ground. The smell was as dry and rotted as the cabin looked. It was like the ground itself was rotting away, and the awful smell permeated everything. They say your nose eventually cancels out a smell after a while, but this one showed no signs of going away. I was on the edge of vomiting for minutes as we slowly and quietly unpacked the trunk of the car.

Afraid? You bet I was. I was moving so slowly and carefully because I was afraid the house would notice me and come roaring to life, so eerie the feel was here. There was no wind, no forest sounds, and no noise of any kind other than our footfalls and the squeaks and groans of Larry's automobile as things were shifted from it to the dead ground.

Larry was mumbling, and Fawn was hanging close to him throughout the unpacking, giving each other comfort and reassurance. Uncle Todd had his jaw clamped closed so hard, the muscles in his cheeks quivered. I think it had to hit him the hardest. Knowing what the place was like now versus what he remembered it as. It had to be hard to see this place turned into such an abomination.

Uncle Todd straightened as he put the plastic tub holding his spell-crafting gear on the ground. He was looking at the cabin, but it was easy to see he was remembering what it used to be. "This was such a great place to come to. Your dad and I stayed here as kids for holidays and summer vacation. Our folks would bring us here. You could run through the woods and see all sorts of things," he said haltingly, a catch in his voice. "There's a lake down the hill behind the cabin where we used to catch fish. The meadow that was on the west side of the lake was the best place to lie down and watch the stars at night." He shook his head sadly, then set his jaw. He looked towards a nearly obscured path that went to the right of the house and into the dead forest.

"The meadow's up that way. That's where the circle is, so that's where we have to go." He looked at me, then over at Fawn and Larry, who were listening with intense interest and a lot of fear mixed together.

Todd shouldered the coils of wire and grabbed the iron stakes to keep the loop of metal grounded. Larry looked at the house, started towards it. Suddenly, we all felt the sense of awareness that emanated from the house. There was something there, or the house itself was aware. Larry felt it too, and his stride towards the house died in dead, dusty mustard-colored mid-step. He backed away very slowly, white with fear, and the presence slowly dissipated as he continued his slow retreat back past the dilapidated car that stood sentinel in the front of the house.

"Okay, that was the creepiest feeling I've had so far," said Larry as he relaxed after getting back to his car. "No more curiosity for this little wizard." The dead, yellow-brown dust slowly settled back to the ground like a soundless 'Amen-brother'.

"Good plan," said Fawn, and she pulled him into a tight, almost desperate hug, that he returned, and held until Todd informed us that we were wasting time.

Larry picked up the sleeping Rynun, and shouted "Jesus Christ!" We spun in unison. Larry was looking at Rynun, who looked like a withered caricature of himself. He remained in the deep sleep he had fallen into when we entered the forest. Now he was a vomit yellow-brown furred *Geowludmosiseg*. He looked as sickly and leprous as the trees. He seemed to be shriveling away as he lay in Larry's arms. I looked at Fawn and she shrugged her shoulders. "I don't know what we can do short stuff. He might get better once we finish the spell."

We shouldered our supplies and I checked my snub-nose revolver. I had taken the time to put a drop of holy water in the tip of each hollow point bullet and cover the end with wax to hold the water in place. I didn't know if it was going to work, but it made me feel better about my chances of being able to shoot Baldy/*Ahiah* and make it stick.

We started along the trail towards the lake, and as we reached the edge of the hill, utter desolation greeted our eyes. The trees had rotted so badly that the only thing left on the top part of the hill were stumps that poked like the ribs of a rotting corpse from the ground. The stumps disappeared halfway down and all you saw was dust to the edge of the lake, or rather, where the lake should have been. Instead of water, there was a blob of something that glistened greasily in the pale light. The thick, leprous yellow brown layer of dust covered everything. Larry kneeled to look at it. "I think it's the trees, it looks like the powdered remains of rotted wood I had to clean out of the store when I first bought it."

As we approached the lake the smell of rotted meat and vegetation hit us like a wall. The miasma from the lake combined with the horrid stench up by the cabin was too much for me. I fell to the ground and puked my guts out. I retched for what felt like minutes and had dry heaves for a minute or two longer, when my body seemed to finally control itself. I felt anger at all this violation. It spread through me like a fire.

I stood up and screamed like a madwoman. Despair and horror twisted into rage and determination. I would not let this refugee from a horror novel ruin this place or mess with me anymore. The others were reacting in much the same way. You get rubbed in something loathsome for so long it begins to lose its ability to cause horror and abhorrence. I was way past that, and all the way to complete disgust. It was not some loathsome, terrifying place any more, it was an open wound that needed to be cauterized.

I heard Rynun sigh, and it seemed like he became a little browner again, as if our determination had helped him a little. Weird. I quit trying to make sense of it and walked determinedly down the hill towards the clearing with the others.

We got to the clearing and felt, more than saw, the suspended spell. It was a slithering pulsation that never hit you the same way twice, like being pushed in every direction at once. I could see at the site where the circle supposedly was, a putrid yellowish glow, then green, and finally a sick, pale brownish-white. That had to be the spell, held in place with the casting unfinished. I'd never seen a spell do that, or even heard of one stopping in mid-cast. The ones I'd heard of either dissipated, or blew up, or any number of unpleasant things, but didn't just sit. Curiosity made me hurry my steps, and then I wished I hadn't.

I saw my parents, and I heard Fawn gasp and choke back a cry. We'd gotten close enough to be able to see past the haze of the spell. We saw Mom and Dad, their bodies withered and brown. They looked like corn husks, their bodies poised in mid-fall and mid-cast.

They were suspended just over two points of a very faint pentagram, and I could see ghostly images of a much younger Uncle Todd, Fawn, and me at the others. We were lying on the points, with bags over our heads. Uncle Todd was caught in mid-stride as he bolted from his point on the pentagram toward Fawn's prone body.

I wasn't certain what to make of the tableau. I didn't know whether to be sick, outraged, or just thankful. Uncle Todd was on his knees in the thick, yellow dust. He was hugging himself, rocking back and forth. How would I, or Fawn react if we were the ones coming back here in Todd's circumstance? I shook my head to clear it. This whole area seemed to just want us to lose ourselves. Everything felt wrong, and we weren't even started on the spell.

Larry walked over to Todd and helped him up. "What did you do to prepare the spell anyway?" he said to him. "I've never heard of one doing something like this. All I ever heard was the disasters that happened when the casting was interrupted."

"It was the warding around the circle. They were supposed to keep the called power contained. I think it kept the magick from blowing sky-high when we ran."

Todd shuddered again as he looked at the circle. Then he straightened and led Larry, Fawn, and me around the circle. He indicated the location of each point of the pentagram and the symbols still barely visible through the dust. Larry still carried Rynun, and I didn't wonder much why. If the area was sucking the life from him, like we guessed it might be, how much worse would it be if he touched the ground?

"I was on the northernmost point," Todd said, and led us to his 'spot' on the circle. He looked so much like the ghost image that it was like looking at twins, only the age lines in Todd's face and the gray hair made the difference. "My position was to take the excess magick and return it to the Pentagram. I was the ground wire so to speak," he concluded.

"Fawn, Fern's and your points were the receivers for the magick that your parents pulled from the entity and channeled to the two of you. That magick was supposed to destroy the disease that was killing you two and return you to life and full health, but when I pulled off the circle, there was no ground and I guess, the best description would be feedback like in a microphone."

"Why aren't we dead then?" I asked him. "If the spell needed us dead and we weren't, how did it cure us?"

Todd shook his head again. "I don't know for certain. You two were on the circle for a good five minutes before I got frightened enough to move. The first part of the spell I think was a purge of some kind, and the second part was to pull power to you to breathe life back into your bodies and kept your souls bound into them as the magick did its job. With you two being alive, I think that was what caused things to go wrong. The entity was in the middle of the circle and he started howling like he was in pain. Come to think of that, where is it? If all of us were caught like a photograph here, why wasn't it?"

Fawn answered that one for me at least, "Hmmm, don't know, don't care. Let's get this done and get out of here," she said.

"I second the motion," Larry said with a weak smile.

Todd walked the perimeter one more time and began directing us to lay a larger circle around the existing circle and spell. We would try to banish it first, and if that didn't work, we'd have to set up everything again to try and complete the spell.

We put the silver wire down, discarding the idea of the cold iron as this was not fey magick from Todd's description. Every six feet or so a stake was driven into the ground to anchor the wire. Larry told us to use the plastic stakes so the silver wire wasn't accidentally magickally grounded.

The points of the pentagram were set opposite the original placement, putting the new points in between the originals. Larry set Fawn and me on opposite sides of Uncle Todd's original point, with himself at the point on my side and the still unconscious Rynun next to Fawn. Rynun gasped as he was laid on the ground and he curled even tighter into a fetal position. Uncle Todd was the last point. I looked at our parents on their points of the original circle. Their bodies remained frozen in place. I wondered what would happen to them when we broke the spell trapping them. I caught Fawn making quick glances at them too. So many things I wanted to know. Now wasn't the time, as much as I wanted it to be. I returned to pounding stakes and stretching the silver with Fawn and Larry.

Now that the circle was set, we had to get the entity to return. Todd quickly led us through the chant that he, Mom, and Dad used the first time. As we started the chant, the whole place got even quieter, like the sounds were swallowed as they were being made. Our voices dropped to whispers even though we were almost shouting. A pressure started to build up and the sickly yellow dust started to rise inside the original circle as if something was moving underneath it.

Sounds became distorted like in a tunnel. Echoes assaulted our ears as a jumble of sound from our own voices. Every word sounded sideways or broken. It was like the speaker had no idea of inflection or how the word was accented. The dust had blurred into a blocky sort of outline that was easily four times as tall as us, and almost completely filled the inner circle. There was movement all around. Puffs of the sickly dust rose up like from footfalls of something unseen stalking around us. As the dust rose, it parted like something running through it.

I started to follow the barely seen movements, and got a yell from Larry and Todd to stand still. "It's the test! The test of fortitude! Don't move! You move they'll attack you!" Uncle Todd screamed. I stood, but every nerve in my body said that these things were here to take us. I was near frantic to defend myself. I managed to clamp down on that instinctive reaction, and held my ground as the sky darkened, and the ground grew soft and unsteady. Uncle Todd managed to yell loud enough to get our attention over the other noise. "Stay on your point, and face inward! Don't let them distract you!"

Easier said than done, but I focused as hard as I could inward towards the rising spiral of dust. I almost didn't see Uncle Todd fall. It was just at the edge of my perception, and I turned slightly towards him. Something had happened and he was collapsing onto the point. Instinctively, I broke from the circle and ran along the edge towards Uncle Todd. Larry yelled something I didn't hear. I got about five steps towards Uncle Todd and was flattened by a blow that hit me in the back. My head smashed against the ground, making my vision jump crazily. I lay stunned and heard Larry and Fawn scream. As I tried to rise, I was hit in the back of the head and there was a great white light, and then darkness.

I awoke back on the original circle, in my original location. I tried to stand up, and the nausea dropped me to my hands and knees. I tried to empty my stomach again. My head throbbed painfully where I'd been hit. There were two images of everything. I guessed I might have a concussion, but wasn't sure. I was yanked to my feet, and held for a moment as the world spun. My visions was filled with a ghastly yellow brown haze. The damnable yellowish dust had been stirred up so much that it was hard to see beyond the far edge of the circle.

The first thing that focused was a large humanoid shape in the center of the circle. It stood there, frozen as if it was trying to pull free of the earth. I saw Uncle Todd past the figure at the north point of the pentacle, and Fawn to my right. We were all in our original spots. I looked towards where Mom and Dad were. The two of them were upright, rather than frozen in mid-fall.

They looked at me from dead, withered bodies that belonged in a zombie horror movie. Their slight movements were as stiff as the wood that they resembled. Fawn was looking over at our parents with an appalled expression. Mom and Dad's gaze turned to me, and I felt my insides turn to jelly. The malignant hunger on their faces scared me spitless. I tried to find Larry and Rynun, but couldn't see them for the dust.

"Looking for your friends?" asked an ugly, familiar voice. The motion to turn and look made me nearly throw up. Larry and Rynun were behind me, away from the pentagram. They were trapped in the same kind of swirling circle of dust that Uncle Todd, Fawn, and I were.

"I must say that you three were very hard to track." Baldy said with a sensual smile on his face as he appeared out of nowhere, and stood next to me. "Your pet wizard was very good at obfuscating your trail until you tried to dismiss this spell." He walked slowly over to Fawn, who grimaced and tried to punch him. Baldy knocked her down with what looked like a tap to her forehead with a single finger. She slammed to the ground with a cry of pain. Baldy chuckled as she woozily tried to find her feet.

"I couldn't let you do that, not when it has been sitting so long waiting to be finished," he said. Baldy/*Ahiah* walked over to Uncle Todd. "Wouldn't you want a chance to finish something in your life after such a long time? A little closure perhaps? A chance to say how sorry you are to run out on your brother and parents?" He quickly walked over to Todd and grabbed him by the back of the neck. I tried to bolt off the circle. Wind sprang up, knocking me to my knees, choking and retching as the hideous dust started suffocating me as I tried to step from my point.

I stood up and watched as he forced Todd to look at his brother and sister-in-law. "Can't you feel the love they send you," he said mockingly. "Can you not see the joy in their eyes as they look upon you after such a long time away? Surely you must have something to say to them," he said in that silky, purring voice, and I saw Todd start to lean back as Baldy squeezed his neck and forced him to look at Mom and Dad.

He held Todd by the neck and marched him over to mom on his toes. "Why don't you give your sister a kiss on the cheek for old-time's sake?" He pushed Todd's face close to Mom. At the last minute, as Todd screamed in agony, Mom's "husk" grabbed Todd's face and bit a huge chunk of his cheek from his face and swallowed it. Baldy held Todd up effortlessly and dragged him over to Dad.

The exact same scene was repeated with Dad digging an extra deep chunk of flesh out of Todd's shoulder. The shriek Todd made sounded like a soul damned. His eyes were glazed in shock when Baldy marched him back across the circle to his point, and the wind surrounding the spot held him upright, bleeding, choking, and retching.

Ahiah/Baldy then sauntered over to Larry and Rynun. Larry was barely conscious. Rynun looked like a desiccated corpse. The place had been taking his life away from him since we brought him here. *Ahiah* looked at the both of them, then lovingly cupped Larry's chin and brought his face close.

"I will enjoy feasting on your soul little wizard, after the spell is cast. Then I will enjoy feeding what's left to my loyal servants," he said in a gloating, mocking tone. He let go of Larry, who fell onto his side. *Ahiah* grinned, then wiggled his fingers towards Mom and Dad, who returned the look with desperate hunger.

He laughed and sauntered back to the center of the circle, and looked at Fawn. "You will be especially tasty," he said. All traces of mockery gone as he faced Fawn. "I will take my time killing you." He turned to me. "And you," he said, crooning hate. "I will make you watch, then I will give you to your loving parents."

"Wow, really, did you think that all up by yourself? Or were you so dumb you needed someone else to tell you how to sound like a villain?" I was mad, and scared. I had a habit of mouthing off when I get like that. It turned out how you think it would. Really bad.

Baldy was on top of me before I could even blink. He held me off the ground by the throat, and grabbed my left hand. Releasing my throat, I was suspended off the ground by the wrist. He took my pinky between thumb and forefinger of his other hand. "It's said that the smallest finger has the most nerve endings. Shall we test it?" he said in a vicious purr, and then bent my finger back until it dislocated. I screamed in agony as he then rotated it and finally tore it off, and then popped it in his mouth and chewed it like a piece of jerky.

My body must have dumped a whole barrel of adrenalin into my system. I never really felt any pain, just a tearing sensation, and the tear where my finger had been barely oozed any blood. He dropped me back on the circle and chuckled as he walked back to the center. I held my hand to myself and tried to protect it from further injury. I didn't want to look at the wound, so I took my shirt off and wrapped the hand with it. I put the silver cross in my bra. Sue me, I'm not a big believer, but I wanted some sort of comfort and that's all I had. "*Ahiah*," I said in as loud a voice as I could, "*Ahiah*, we know who you are!" He stopped momentarily, and looked at me. "So very clever of you, is that what you wanted to hear?" he said mockingly.

He reached into his pocket and pulled the bottle out. He tilted it over his mouth and something golden, like honey fell from the bottle to his lips. *Ahiah* swallowed, and threw the bottle to the side. It landed near Uncle Todd, who tried to shrink away from the thing. A pressure pulsed outward from *Ahiah*. Suddenly he felt way more powerful, and way more terrifying. He laughed like a cheesy comic villain, but there wasn't anything funny about it. *Ahiah* giggled maniacally at Uncle Todd's reaction to the bottle, then turned to look at me, then Fawn. "Let us dispense with the drama and get to the core of the matter shall we?" he said with a vicious mocking tone.

He began to chant and all of us were pulled upright at the start of it. Uncle Todd was swaying, his blood had soaked his shirt and the ground around him as he bled from his wounds. My shirt was starting to soak through with blood. I could feel my hand start to throb as the adrenalin began to wear off.

I saw Fawn try to fight free and get to Larry as *Ahiah* continued the chant. I could just barely see Todd drop into a sitting position. His head slumped forward as his blood started to float around him. I forced my head to turn and glanced at Larry and Rynun. Rynun was almost covered by the dust. Larry was on his knees next to the little brown man. He slowly piled some more dust on Rynun. He trickled some water from a flask. Then *Ahiah's* spell started to access power. It was like being hit with a wall current. My muscles locked up and something started to flow into me.

I was lifted out of my body. I could see it locked rigid by the spell. There was something else here too, an entity that looked like me, but wasn't. Its head and shoulders were just above the ground. The rest of him was still in the ground, and the earth seemed to be trying to pull it back into itself.

I will be reborn now, and you will be held helpless while I devour your world, said the thing. *I will take you and your sister's place, as was intended, I will get my power back, and I WILL be free!* It reached for me and I slapped its 'hands' to the side and followed with a straight punch, just like in self-defense class. The entity fell back, shocked, and I felt a warm glow over my heart. I looked down and the silver cross Larry put on me was glowing. The thing howled even louder and I fell back into my body as the spell eased. *Ahiah* looked at us in hatred and slowed his chant, and the whole spell seemed to slow down with him.

We were still trapped however, and *Ahiah* walked over to me, still chanting, and pulled at the silver chain around my neck. The cross flipped out of my bra, and glowed like a small sun. *Ahiah* hissed in rage and tore the cross from me and flung it beyond the circle. His hand smoked and bubbled where it had made contact.

The spell almost collapsed at that point. *Ahiah* restarted the chant. While he was calling power, Uncle Todd seized the moment and staggered away from his point. The spell began to unravel again as *Ahiah* broke from the circle and grabbed Todd by the neck and leg. He trotted back over to the point on the circle and threw Todd down, then almost as an afterthought, straightened Uncle Todd's left leg and then kicked it hard on the side, causing the leg to flop at a right angle to the body and tearing every ligament in the knee.

Todd screamed and fell back on the blood-soaked ground, unable to rise. *Ahiah* looked at Fawn and me, then stalked over to Fawn. Fawn tried knee him, but was picked up by the throat and shaken. He used his other hand to rip her shirt open. She had her silver cross. *Ahiah* hissed as it started to glow. He grasped the chain and tore it loose, then flung it away.

Dropping Fawn, he stalked back to the center of the circle, and said, "Can we please finish this fucking spell this time? I'm really getting tired of these interruptions. Mike and Cathy haven't eaten in ages. They're practically, well, completely skin and bones!" *Ahiah* laughed at his own joke and began the chant again.

I looked back over at Larry. He sat alone in the green grass next to a depression in the ground. I didn't see Rynun. I looked around and then back at Larry. Grass! As I watched, a low, thin line of grass appeared through the dust and slowly crept towards me. The grass stopped for a moment, then a line of grass sprouted into the circle. The dust devil around me collapsed. I was able to move!

I didn't run right away like Uncle Todd did. I managed to keep myself from moving outside the point I was on. The grass grew beneath my feet and bent towards my legs and brushed there, and the throbbing pain in my hand ceased like a light switch turning off.

A stone knife pushed itself out of the fresh earth and lay on the ground next to my feet. I felt, rather than heard Rynun. *Use my knife, and strike true. You'll know when.* Rynun then burrowed towards Fawn directly across the circle. *Ahiah* saw the line of fresh grass. I felt the spell falter slightly as *Ahiah* slowed the chant so he could move after Rynun.

Wherever he trod, the grass withered, cutting off the head of the green from the existing line. The grass behind *Ahiah* began to wither back towards Larry, turning brown and withering and crumbling to gray-yellow detritus, and then to dust. The lead portion, where Rynun was, still crawled forward towards Fawn.

Fawn tried to step back from *Ahiah*, but a negligent flick of his hand brought a surging whirlwind of choking dust around her. She fell to her hands and knees, coughing and dry-heaving.

Ahiah walked around to the front of the grass line and placed a foot in front of it, still chanting. The grass line grew right up to his foot, and then tried to slide around it. *Ahiah* stomped the circle of growing grass and a faint scream could be heard coming from below ground.

Rynun emerged from the earth and tried to crawl away from *Ahiah*, who followed with a smile of pure malevolence directed at the rapidly aging *Geowludmosiseg*. The little Brown Man threw a feeble punch at *Ahiah*, and he was slammed to the earth by a gesture. Bending down, *Ahiah* reached to pick up Rynun with his back to me.

I stepped as quickly as I could from the point of the pentagram and ran towards *Ahiah*. *Ahiah* picked Rynun up and placed the bottle on his cheek just as I reached him. I threw my whole body behind the knife as I stabbed upward. He had heard me coming at the last minute and turned slightly so I missed his back and stabbed deep into his right side up under the ribs.

My momentum carried me into him and we crashed to the ground in a heap. I felt the spell weaken further with the slight gasping utterance from *Ahiah*. Fawn shouted at something and I heard a quick shuffling and saw Larry grab *Ahiah*'s shoulders and pull him away from me. *Ahiah* twisted his hand, and I heard Rynun scream. The ground shriveled and cracked. Larry pulled *Ahiah* upright and I saw blood spurt from the stab wound. *Ahiah* didn't act like he was hurt. He responded and grasped Larry's wrist and squeezed. I heard Larry scream as his wrist crackled and snapped.

There was a loud report, and *Ahiah* jerked upright as a burst of blood and flesh erupted from his neck as the bullet tore through it. Rynun screamed louder. I turned and saw his body turn a sickly yellow. He flopped over in agony. I saw the glass bottle, attached to his side. It was sucking his essence.

179

Fawn shot *Ahiah* again. His roar of pain was deafening. I reached over and slapped the bottle on Rynun's waist, my skin crawling as the bottle flipped away with a gurgle and a sucking sound. Fawn saw the bottle and fired, earth kicking up next to it, and skidding it across the sick ground. Rynun collapsed, weeping. I pulled my snub nose and fired. I pulled the shot wide. The change in *Ahiah* was immediate. He charged towards me screaming.

Larry fell to his side clutching his ears. Fawn crumpled to one knee, trying to aim and cover her ears at the same time. A shot kicked up dirt next to me. I rolled away trying to shut out the noise and get clear. *Ahiah* turned to face her at the sound. Fawn steadied herself as *Ahiah* re-started his charge. The first shot missed, hitting something that landed near me with a soft thud. Fawn's second shot caught him in the stomach and folded him over. *Ahiah* crumpled to the ground. Before we'd even caught our breaths, he was back up. I tried to get up and the earth and sky spun crazily. My hand brushed the object that landed by me. It was the stone knife.

Use it now! Don't let him get to the bottle! The words exploded inside my head, making the earth spin faster. I heard an impact and saw *Ahiah* flip and fall as Fawn shot him down again. She stepped back, as *Ahiah* lurched off the ground at her.

I oriented on the bottle. *Ahiah* was trying to grab Fawn. She dodged to her right, and saw me stagger towards the bottle. *Ahiah* noticed too, and immediately came at me screaming and growling like an insane animal. Fawn put two bullets into him, thigh and lower back. They barely slowed him down. He was going to get me. I mumbled a quick prayer and tossed the blade. It sailed end-over-end and actually caught *Ahiah* just above the knee point first. It did what bullets couldn't. He fell, clutching at his leg and screaming. Something in the ground roared in hate and frustration. I felt, more than heard the sound.

I got to the bottle and picked it up. *Break it! Use the blade and break it!* Uh oh. Fawn had gotten to me. The world spun. The adrenalin was wearing off. My body started trying to shut down and escape the pain. "Got to get the knife," I said woozily. "Got to break bottle with knife." I couldn't talk coherently. The stub of my torn finger felt like it was dipped in fire. The pain was the only thing keeping me awake.

"Stay here Shorty," Fawn said to me and ran to where *Ahiah* was trying to pull the knife out of his leg. She kicked him in the head as hard as she could, and that seemed to stun him. She leaned over and yanked the stone knife free in a spurt of blood. *Ahiah* animated immediately and began to stand up.

Fawn tossed me the knife and was slammed flat by *Ahiah*. The knife fell next to me. As I fumbled trying to pick it up, I heard a thud, and a second one. I got the knife and raised it. I heard a scream as *Ahiah* saw what I was about to do.

"Screw you ugly!" I brought the knife down on the bottle, shattering it into pieces. *Ahiah* wailed like a damned soul. Everything disappeared in a hurricane of dust and the smell of pine.

19

I DON'T REMEMBER ANYTHING ELSE except Fawn waking me up in the hospital. She was sitting next to my bed, looking at a wedding magazine and talking inanely about wedding plans. I listened for a few minutes about how the dresses were going to be a salmon and green color, how Larry was going to be in a traditional black tuxedo for the wedding, how the bridesmaids would have matching corsages, rather than bouquets. It was so sickeningly sweet I couldn't take any more.

"Ah god Fawn, I hate the colors," I said, or at least tried to. My voice came out as a dry croak, but it startled Fawn and she jumped to her feet. "Shorty! You're awake! Oh thank god!" she said, hugging me, crying and laughing all at the same time. "We didn't know if you were going to wake up at all. You've been in a coma for three weeks."

"Three weeks?! What happened?" I croaked. I sounded like a frog left three days in the desert. "When did I get here?"

"We brought you here after the magick you turned loose settled out," she replied.

"I think I saw *Ahiah* get pulled into the ground by a hand." She paused as she thought back. "I heard him screaming 'No, Father!' over and over. Then he just disappeared." She paused and looked at me. "The stuff you let loose from the bottle covered the whole place. It started raining. Rynun started laughing. He was dancing in the rain as it fell. Grass, flowers, and other green things were growing wherever he stepped. It was incredible!" she said, a sense of wonder in her voice.

She looked down at me. "You were awake, and delirious. Larry and I got you and Uncle Todd to the car. As Larry started the car, Rynun came over and handed me that stone knife. He told me to give it to you when you woke up." Her excited smile faded as she spoke. "Uncle Todd was in bad shape from all the blood loss, he died on the way to the hospital. Mom and Dad crumbled away when you broke the bottle and *Ahiah* disappeared."

I went numb when she told me about Uncle Todd. I suppose it was balance of a sort. He helped build the circle that let *Ahiah* loose. But I wished I could have seen him again. There was an emptiness in my heart. Zhirk, and Uncle Todd. I wanted to cry, but something wouldn't let me. I think I'd fought so long to lock the pain away, I didn't know how to let it go. Fawn was still talking, and her voice slowly drew me back out of myself.

"...be stiff but he says he got off lucky. He gets the cast off in another four weeks, and then he gets to start therapy for it."

"What about Rynun? He's okay, isn't he?" I asked Fawn.

"Yes, he's living out there at the lake now. Says he got his life back when we broke the bottle."

"What about Zhirk then? Did he come back?" I asked quickly. If Rynun got better, then maybe Zhirk did.

Fawn saddened and said, "No Fernie. He's gone just like that creep Hervald, and all those people that got sucked into that effing bottle. They're gone. I'm sorry Fern."

It was then that the emotions finally woke up. The numbness burst into an aching loss, and I cried uncontrollably for a while. Fawn cried too, hugging and rocking me until I was able to pull myself together. We talked for a little bit and then the nurse came in. She immediately called for the doctor, who came striding in. With a professional smile plastered on his face, he checked me over. "Looking good for three weeks of IV and stomach pumping." He glanced at the chart. "Start with soup and ground up food. Your stomach's shrunk so eating's going to be difficult for a few days. I'm also assigning you physical therapy. Three times a week for two weeks. Get those unused muscles back in proper tone."

Rynun had left a message for me and Fawn in the knife. He told us we had portions of *Ahiah*'s power, and that until we could release it and send it back to him, he would have a toehold in this world. Apparently we can't touch it, but it's there.

My hand finally healed and I've gotten pretty used to not having that finger. It does ache once in a while. Fawn's wedding happened a month after I got out of the hospital. The dresses were salmon and green. Ugh. After the wedding she told me she was pregnant! Waaaay too much information, but in a good way. I'm hoping they name the baby Zhirk.

YOU MIGHT ALSO ENJOY

Broken Bridge
Book Two of the Glass Bottles Series

by J Dark

Sometimes a broken bridge has to be crossed.

GRIMAULKIN

by L. A. Jacob

Treading the straight and narrow is not natural to one who summons demons.

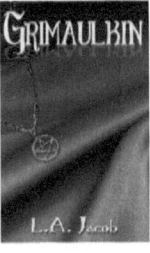

HOMECOMING
A War Mage Novel

by Jake Logan

Even wizards in the U.S. armed forces have to go home some time.

www.ingramcontent.com/pod-product-compliance
Lightning Source LLC
Chambersburg PA
CBHW020437180626
46812CB00003B/1273